BIRD OF PREY

Joe rolled down the window of the van and gazed up at the plane. Suddenly the landing gear descended from the Mustang. "Now what?" Joe muttered as the plane's nose dipped.

When the plane swooped down in front of the van, Frank veered to the side of the road and slammed on the brakes. "Get out!" he shouted.

Joe and Frank ran into the field beside the road and fell to their stomachs. An instant later, the Mustang thundered over the van. The wheels of the plane connected with the roof, and the van tipped over and crashed onto its side.

Joe got up and shook his fist at the airplane. "Come down and fight us face-to-face, you coward!"

"Get down!" Frank yelled, pulling Joe into the grass. The wind from the propeller threw grass and dirt into the air, and the wheels were so low they almost skidded across Joe's back.

"We're trapped!" Frank shouted. "The van is out of commission and there's nowhere to hide!"

Books in THE HARDY BOYS CASEFILES™ Series

#1 DEAD ON TARGET
#2 EVIL, INC.
#3 CULT OF CRIME
#4 THE LAZARUS PLOT
#5 EDGE OF DESTRUCTION
#6 THE CROWNING TERROR
#7 DEATHGAME
#8 SEE NO EVIL
#9 THE GENIUS THIEVES
#10 HOSTAGES OF HATE
#11 BROTHER AGAINST BROTHER
#12 PERFECT GETAWAY
#13 THE BORGIA DAGGER
#14 TOO MANY TRAITORS
#15 BLOOD RELATIONS
#16 LINE OF FIRE
#17 THE NUMBER FILE
#18 A KILLING IN THE MARKET
#19 NIGHTMARE IN ANGEL CITY
#20 WITNESS TO MURDER
#21 STREET SPIES
#22 DOUBLE EXPOSURE
#23 DISASTER FOR HIRE
#24 SCENE OF THE CRIME
#25 THE BORDERLINE CASE
#26 TROUBLE IN THE PIPELINE
#27 NOWHERE TO RUN
#28 COUNTDOWN TO TERROR
#29 THICK AS THIEVES
#30 THE DEADLIEST DARE
#31 WITHOUT A TRACE
#32 BLOOD MONEY
#33 COLLISION COURSE
#34 FINAL CUT
#35 THE DEAD SEASON
#36 RUNNING ON EMPTY
#37 DANGER ZONE
#38 DIPLOMATIC DECEIT

#39 FLESH AND BLOOD
#40 FRIGHT WAVE
#41 HIGHWAY ROBBERY
#42 THE LAST LAUGH
#43 STRATEGIC MOVES
#44 CASTLE FEAR
#45 IN SELF-DEFENSE
#46 FOUL PLAY
#47 FLIGHT INTO DANGER
#48 ROCK 'N' REVENGE
#49 DIRTY DEEDS
#50 POWER PLAY
#51 CHOKE HOLD
#52 UNCIVIL WAR
#53 WEB OF HORROR
#54 DEEP TROUBLE
#55 BEYOND THE LAW
#56 HEIGHT OF DANGER
#57 TERROR ON TRACK
#58 SPIKED!
#59 OPEN SEASON
#60 DEADFALL
#61 GRAVE DANGER
#62 FINAL GAMBIT
#63 COLD SWEAT
#64 ENDANGERED SPECIES
#65 NO MERCY
#66 THE PHOENIX EQUATION
#67 LETHAL CARGO
#68 ROUGH RIDING
#69 MAYHEM IN MOTION
#70 RIGGED FOR REVENGE
#71 REAL HORROR
#72 SCREAMERS
#73 BAD RAP
#74 ROAD PIRATES
#75 NO WAY OUT
#76 TAGGED FOR TERROR
#77 SURVIVAL RUN
#78 THE PACIFIC CONSPIRACY
#79 DANGER UNLIMITED

Available from ARCHWAY Paperbacks

THE HARDY BOYS NO. 79
CASEFILES

DANGER UNLIMITED

FRANKLIN W. DIXON

AN ARCHWAY PAPERBACK
Published by POCKET BOOKS
New York   London   Toronto   Sydney   Tokyo   Singapore

AN ARCHWAY PAPERBACK *Original*

An Archway Paperback published by
POCKET BOOKS, a division of Simon & Schuster Inc.
1230 Avenue of the Americas, New York, NY 10020

Copyright © 1993 by Simon & Schuster Inc.
Produced by Mega-Books of New York, Inc.

ISBN: 0-671-79463-9

First Archway Paperback printing September 1993

10 9 8 7 6 5 4 3 2 1

THE HARDY BOYS, AN ARCHWAY PAPERBACK and colophon are registered trademarks of Simon & Schuster Inc.

THE HARDY BOYS CASEFILES is a trademark of Simon & Schuster Inc.

Cover art by Brian Kotzky

Printed in the U.S.A.

IL 6+

Chapter

1

"COME ON, FRANK, can't we at least stop for breakfast?" Joe Hardy asked his older brother. "I'm starving."

Frank Hardy tapped the brakes of the brothers' customized black van and turned down a side road that led to the outskirts of Bayport. "No way," he replied, glancing over at Joe. "We're late already."

"That's right," said Joe's girlfriend from the backseat. Vanessa Bender brushed a lock of her long, ash-blond hair over her shoulder. "Uncle Brett told Mom that if we want to see his new airplane, we have to meet him behind hangar five at exactly eight A.M."

Joe yawned and ran his hands through his blond hair. "Who is this Brett Cooper guy, anyway? And what's so special about his plane?"

"That's what you get for refusing to talk to me on the phone last night," Vanessa said. "I explained the whole story to your brother."

"Sorry. *Dogfight Over London* was on cable, and I couldn't take my eyes off it. What a great movie!"

Frank shrugged. "Movies are okay, but this is real. We're going to get a firsthand look at a plane that can fly over four hundred fifty miles per hour!"

"No kidding?" Joe was paying attention now. "Okay," he said. "Start from the beginning and tell me what's going on."

Frank turned left, past a sign that read Bayport Airfield, 1 Mile. "Vanessa's mom knows Brett Cooper from back when she was in college," he said. "She signed up for flying lessons, and he was her instructor."

"In fact, Uncle Brett introduced my mom to my dad," Vanessa added. "He and Dad were best friends from their air force days."

"So he's not really your uncle," Joe said.

Vanessa shook her head. "Just an old family friend. I've known him since I was a baby."

"Cooper went on to become one of the top race pilots in the world," Frank continued. "I used to read about him in flying magazines. Five years ago he started working on a new plane. A

year later, he suddenly dropped out of sight—
and no one knows why."

"He's been living like a hermit on a farm in
western Pennsylvania," Vanessa told Joe.
"When he hit town last week, he called Mom
and invited her for lunch. It was the first time
they'd seen each other in almost four years. The
weird thing is, when she asked him what he'd
been doing, he wouldn't answer. That's totally
unlike him, from what I remember. And to tell
you the truth, Mom's kind of worried."

"Hmm," Joe said, "sounds mysterious."

Joe and Frank were always interested in a
good mystery. It was a trait they'd inherited
from their father, Fenton Hardy, a former New
York City police officer who had gone on to become a famous private detective. Although
Frank was only eighteen, and Joe was a year
younger, the brothers had investigated and solved
crimes all over the world. Their active life kept
them in top shape. Dark-haired Frank was a lean
six feet one, and his blond brother was an inch
shorter and more muscular.

"But now Cooper is back with a new plane
that he says will beat the piston-engine world
speed record," Frank said. "He plans to unveil
it at the Bayport air races tomorrow."

"The plane is top secret," Vanessa added.
"But I knew you two would love to get a close-
up look, so I asked Mom to put in a good word

with Uncle Brett." She gave Frank a friendly shove. "You owe me one, guys."

"Hey, look at that!" Joe cried suddenly, peering through the windshield.

Frank's head snapped up. Flying toward them, at an altitude of no more than three hundred feet, was a red fighter plane with black wing stripes. Its high-powered piston engine roared like a ferocious lion.

"Awesome!" Frank exclaimed. "It's a World War II Grumman F8F-2 Bearcat. There aren't many of those still flying."

Joe chuckled. He could never get over how much Frank knew about airplanes. Frank even had his pilot's license.

Joe's thoughts were cut short when he noticed the Bearcat's nose suddenly dip downward. "Hey, it's heading right toward us!" he shouted.

The plane plunged through the sky, gaining speed as it fell. The nose was pointed straight at Joe and Frank's van. "It's going to crash!" Vanessa cried.

Frank jerked the van's steering wheel sharply and swerved off the road into an empty field. Glancing back, he read the words painted across the Bearcat's side: *Killer Diller*.

No sooner had they bounced to a stop than the Bearcat's nose leveled off and the plane zoomed over their heads. As it gained altitude and circled back toward the airport, Frank said, "Friends, we've just been buzzed."

Joe jumped out of the van. He stared up at the departing airplane. "You mean that idiot pilot was just trying to scare us?" he asked.

"Looks that way," Vanessa replied.

Joe scowled. "Who would do something that stupid?"

"We'll find out," Frank said. He checked his watch. "Oh, man, we've only got three minutes to make it to hangar five."

Joe leaped back into the van. "Step on it," he said.

The airfield, which lay about five miles outside of town, was bigger than many private ones. There were several hangars, a small pilots' clubhouse, and a single runway. Frank, Joe, and Vanessa drove into the airfield's parking lot and jogged north toward the hangars. A sign over the clubhouse said Welcome to the Bayport Unlimited Air Races.

"I knew the airfield put on an annual air show," Joe said, "but since when do they sponsor air races, too?"

"This is the first year," Frank answered. "Some airfields, like the one in Reno, Nevada, host all four race classes—biplanes, Formula Ones, AT-6s, and Unlimiteds. The Bayport Airfield is too small to handle all those planes, so they opted to host just an Unlimited race."

"What does Unlimited mean?" Joe asked.

"The only qualifications are that the planes must be propeller driven and powered by piston engines," Frank explained. "Otherwise, anything goes."

"Was that Bearcat an Unlimited racer?" Joe asked. "That thing could really move!"

Frank nodded. "All of the planes are World War II fighters with clipped wings and huge souped-up engines. Every year there's talk of someone developing a brand-new piston-powered plane that can beat the Bearcats and Mustangs, but so far it hasn't happened."

"Maybe this is the year," Vanessa said. "If Uncle Brett's plane is all he says it is— Oh!" she exclaimed. "There's Uncle Brett now!" Vanessa walked quickly toward a large, forty-year-old bear of a man with brown hair and a mustache. He was wearing grease-stained orange coveralls, cowboy boots, and a white cap with the words *Brett's Beauty* across the front.

"You just made it," Cooper said gruffly. He inhaled on the unfiltered cigarette he held in his grease- and tobacco-stained hands. "A couple more seconds and I would have been out of here."

Vanessa put her hands on her hips. "Well, that's a nice way to greet someone you haven't seen in five whole years."

Cooper looked at her and his scowling face softened. "Looks like Harry Bender's little girl grew up," he said with a rough laugh.

Vanessa smiled and let herself be swallowed

up in a massive hug. "Uncle Brett," she said, "these are my friends, Frank and Joe Hardy."

"We would have been here sooner, Mr. Cooper," Joe said, "but some wiseguy in a red Bearcat tried to take our heads off."

"A red Bearcat? That would be Cameron Diller," Cooper said, practically spitting out the name.

Frank nodded. "His plane is called the *Killer Diller*, right?"

"Young hotshot," Cooper muttered. "Only twenty-one years old and he thinks he knows everything. But when the time trials start tomorrow, he'll learn different."

"We appreciate you taking the time to show us your new plane," Frank said. "You must be busy."

"I am," Cooper snapped. "I'll tell you the truth, if it weren't for my friendship with Andrea Bender, I wouldn't be doing this. This plane is top secret."

"We understand," Joe said.

"No, you don't. This plane isn't simply going to win the Unlimited race and set a new speed record. It's going to revolutionize small-aircraft aviation."

Frank's eyes lit up. "Lead the way," he said eagerly.

"The plane isn't here," Cooper replied. "It's under wraps until I unveil it tomorrow. I'm going to drive you to it." He pointed to a muddy red Jeep Cherokee parked beside the hangar.

Frank climbed into the front seat while Joe and Vanessa got in the back. During the long drive, Frank noticed that Cooper said very little, but concentrated instead on the complex, circuitous route he was taking. Clearly, Cooper intended to confuse his passengers so they couldn't find his hangar if they tried to come back.

But Frank watched carefully, memorizing the route. He also studied Cooper. As the pilot drove, he constantly checked the rearview mirrors.

"Has anyone ever tried to follow you out here?" Frank asked.

"Not yet, but I'm not taking any chances," Cooper answered curtly. "Unlimited air racing isn't exactly a gentleman's sport. Just last year, a fellow from Cameron Diller's pit crew was caught tampering with another pilot's engine."

As he spoke, Cooper turned off the road and drove down a long dirt driveway. Frank estimated that they had traveled approximately fifteen miles from the airfield. Cooper stopped in front of an old Quonset hut—a prefabricated shelter of corrugated metal with an arching roof. It was surrounded by open fields and, beyond the fields, dense woods. The original doors of the hut had been replaced with doors large enough for a small aircraft to fit through.

Cooper unlocked the doors and led Frank, Joe, and Vanessa inside the unlit building. "The future of the piston-powered engine," he boomed. "I give you *Brett's Beauty*."

Cooper flipped on the lights to reveal a sleek white airplane with an all-composite twin-boom design. Frank stared in amazement. The center cockpit, flanked by two booms, each with its own engine and propeller, made *Brett's Beauty* look more like a flying catamaran than a traditional airplane. But it was the size of the plane that surprised Frank the most. The *Beauty* was so small that its highest point wouldn't even reach a Bearcat's wingtip. Frank estimated the airplane was no more than thirty feet long, with a wing span of only thirty or forty feet.

"So this is what you've been up to at that little farm in Pennsylvania," Vanessa said.

"I sure wasn't growing corn." Cooper chuckled. "I built her in my barn and did the test flights right there. Her first long flight was from the farm to here, and she handled like a dream."

"And this little plane can outrun Cameron Diller's Bearcat?" Frank asked with amazement.

"You better believe it," Cooper said. "With a good tailwind, the *Beauty* can break five hundred miles an hour."

Joe grinned. "Outrageous."

"See, my plan was to forget about those World War II planes and start with a clean slate, using the latest available technology," Cooper said, warming to his subject. "I minimized the frontal area of the plane and kept the aerodynamic drag to an absolute minimum."

"That's why she's so fast," Frank said.

"But this baby isn't just about speed," Cooper continued. "What's really amazing about the *Beauty* is her efficiency. Lower drag means less engine horsepower and less fuel, and that means less pollution. Plus, she's cheaper to run," Cooper added. "My plane can go twice as far on a tank of fuel as the average Cessna 150."

"What's that computer for?" Joe asked, motioning to a computer terminal in the corner of the room.

"The *Beauty* is entirely computer controlled," Cooper answered. "We can hook up that terminal to the engines and check out the whole system in minutes."

"I see what you mean about this plane revolutionizing small-aircraft aviation," Vanessa said. "Your design could be adapted for all kinds of small planes—fire planes, military planes, even cargo planes."

"But so far it's all theoretical, right?" Joe asked. "I mean, you'll have to wait until the race to know for sure if you can really outfly the big guns."

"I'll dust 'em," Cooper shot back. "Hey," he said, suddenly smiling, "you want a real thrill? Let me start her up. The engines sound like a leopard's purr."

He lifted the canopy and climbed into the small, two-seat cockpit. Joe, Frank, and Vanessa stood to the left of the cockpit and watched as Cooper flipped some switches. Within seconds, the engine roared to life. The *Beauty* wailed, straining at the cords that bound the right and left tail boom to the floor.

"Well," he shouted over the twin engines' roar, "what do you think?"

At that moment, the left engine sputtered and coughed.

"Is that normal?" Joe shouted. But Cooper didn't answer. He was flipping switches on the blinking control panel of the plane.

And then the cough switched to a deafening high-pitched whine. Either something was going very wrong with the plane's engine, or Cooper had invented a real jalopy of a bird, Frank thought.

"Uncle Brett," Vanessa was shouting, "is everything okay?"

Cooper frantically gestured to the propeller in front of them, but his words were drowned out by a loud crack. It was the left propeller. Somehow it had snapped off the plane! In the next second its knife-sharp steel blades were whizzing right at their heads!

"Hit the ground!" Frank cried, as the revolving wheel of death shot out at them.

Chapter

2

OUT OF THE CORNER of his eye, Joe saw Vanessa fall to her knees. With lightning speed, he threw himself on top of her, protecting her with his body.

Frank dropped to the floor an instant later. As he fell, the airplane's left propeller whizzed over his head, missing him by mere inches and ripping a large hole in the side of the Quonset hut.

A second later, Joe heard the *Beauty*'s engine sputter and die. "You kids all right?" Cooper asked, jumping out of the cockpit.

"I think so," Vanessa said in a small voice.

"Man, that thing could have taken our heads off!" Joe said as he helped Vanessa up.

"What happened, Mr. Cooper?" Frank asked.

But Cooper didn't answer. Instead, he turned and strode purposefully through the doors of the Quonset hut. Joe followed him and saw that after bursting through the wall, the propeller had smashed into the hard-packed soil.

"It's ruined," Cooper muttered angrily. "As if I weren't broke already . . ."

Ignoring Joe, Cooper walked back into the building. Joe followed him to find Frank and Vanessa standing beside the *Beauty*'s left nose.

"Mr. Cooper," Frank said, "I think I've found the cause of the problem. Take a look."

Frank handed Cooper the remains of the large main bolt that had once held the propeller in place. It was a mangled mess, as were the smaller bolts and wires that were still partially attached to the nose.

"Pot metal!" Cooper said gruffly, examining the bolt.

"What's that?" Vanessa asked.

"A soft, cheap metal used for car trim, toys, things like that," Frank explained. "It's not nearly strong enough to hold an airplane propeller in place."

Joe knew that could mean only one thing—sabotage. "Any thoughts on who might want to damage the *Beauty?*" he asked Cooper.

"Everybody," the pilot replied, pulling a pack of unfiltered cigarettes from the pocket of his coveralls. "But it doesn't make sense. I haven't told anyone where I'm storing her."

"What about your pit crew?" Frank asked. "Couldn't someone have followed one of them here?"

Cooper lit a cigarette and shook his head. "The crew members are staying in a trailer out back. None of them has been to Bayport since we arrived."

"What about you?" Joe asked.

"I went to the airfield to register for the races, that's all. And believe me, I kept an eye out to make sure no one followed me."

"Are you sure you can trust the pit crew guys?" Frank asked.

"I don't trust anyone," Cooper shot back. "Not anymore."

"What do you mean, Uncle Brett?" Vanessa asked. "Has something like this happened before?"

Frank answered for him. "Mr. Cooper, I'm a big fan of air racing. Didn't I read a few years back about someone breaking into your barn in Pennsylvania and smashing your plane's engine with a sledgehammer?"

"Wow," Joe said, his eyes widening. "Do you think it could have been done by the same person?"

Cooper shrugged and looked away.

"Uncle Brett," Vanessa said, "why are you being so closemouthed? Maybe Joe and Frank can help you."

Cooper laughed grimly. "You expect me to

14

believe a couple of teenagers can track down the person who tampered with this propeller?''

"Joe and Frank Hardy aren't just any teenagers," Vanessa insisted. "They're detectives. They've solved dozens of crimes."

"Give us a try, Mr. Cooper," Frank said. "What have you got to lose?"

"I don't need your help, or anyone else's," Cooper snapped. "Besides, when the races are over, everyone in the world will know what *Brett's Beauty* can do. The airplane companies will be begging me to design planes for them. I'll be rolling in money, and the last four years will seem like nothing but a bad dream."

Frank frowned. Joe glanced at Vanessa, who looked stunned.

Before she could say a word, the doors flew open and Joe saw a small man in greasy jeans and a denim shirt burst into the room. He was in his early twenties, with a long nose and thin brown mustache that made him look like a large rat.

"What happened?" he asked, nervously running his hands through his tousled hair. Then suddenly, he noticed Frank, Joe, and Vanessa. "Who are you?"

"Calm down, Ray," Brett said. "This is Vanessa Bender, the daughter of my old air force pal, Harry. And these are a couple of her friends, Frank and Joe Hardy. I brought them out to see the *Beauty*."

The small man forced a smile to his troubled face. "I'm Ray Kolinsky," he said. "Number one man on the *Beauty*'s pit crew." He looked at Cooper. "What's going on, Brett?"

The two men immediately launched into an intense discussion about the damaged propeller. Frank motioned for Joe and Vanessa to follow him outside.

"Uncle Brett is hiding something," Joe said.

Vanessa frowned. "He seems so angry and suspicious," she said with concern. "That's not the Uncle Brett I remember."

"What did he used to be like?" Frank asked.

"Well, he was always a loner. He likes to do things his way or not at all. And that gruff manner of his was always there, only not so pronounced. But deep down, he's a sweetheart. My mom says his wife, Dixie, used to call him a grizzly bear with a marshmallow center."

"Does he have any enemies?" Joe asked.

"I don't know. Maybe. My mom says he was always outspoken, even in the old days. But he never seemed very concerned about what people thought of him."

"Let's take a look around," Frank suggested. "Maybe we can find some clues to tell us who sabotaged that propeller."

Frank set off around the left side of the Quonset hut, while Joe and Vanessa walked around the right side.

Joe paused at a pair of cowboy boot footprints, then dismissed them. They were obviously made by Cooper. Vanessa walked ahead and picked up a crumpled cigarette package from the ground and handed it to Joe.

"That's Cooper's brand," Joe said.

"Funny—I don't remember Uncle Brett smoking," Vanessa said thoughtfully. "I'm surprised his wife stands for it. She was always into health and fitness."

Joe and Vanessa rounded the back of the Quonset hut. Joe spotted the pit crew's trailer in an open field about fifty yards behind the hut. Three cars and a small motor home were parked beside it.

As Joe looked the cars over, he noticed the sun reflecting off an object on the dashboard of a beat-up green Honda wagon. He opened the car door and found a large bolt on the dashboard. It was just like the one used to secure the propeller, only this one was made of steel.

"Frank!" Joe called, climbing out of the car. "Vanessa, go get Mr. Cooper, will you?"

Frank appeared a moment later, followed by Vanessa, Brett Cooper, and Ray Kolinsky. Joe held the bolt in the palm of his hand for everyone to see.

"The propeller bolt!" Cooper cried angrily.

"Whose car is this?" Joe asked.

"It's mine," Kolinsky admitted. "But I never—"

"You did this!" Cooper shouted. "This is the last straw!"

"Brett," Kolinsky protested, "you know I'd never hurt the *Beauty*. Besides, if I did switch the bolts, do you think I'd be dumb enough to put the old one in my car for everyone to see? It's a setup!"

Cooper hesitated. Joe watched as the pilot stared suspiciously at Ray, then frowned uncertainly.

"What Ray says makes sense," Frank ventured. "And that means that whoever did sabotage the plane could still be around."

At that moment, the trailer door opened. The other two pit crew members, a short, stocky, freckled man and a barrel-chested, dark-skinned man stepped out to see what was going on. Their presence seemed to make Cooper angry all over again.

"When I want your opinion, I'll ask for it," Cooper roared at Frank. Then, looking as if he'd made up his mind about something, he turned to Kolinsky. "I don't need you. After the Championship Gold race, I won't need anyone. Get your stuff and get out of here!"

Kolinsky stood, stunned, as Cooper said to Vanessa, "You and your friends come with me. I'm taking you back to the airfield."

During the drive to the airfield, Frank thought about what had happened. It seemed odd for Cooper to have fired Ray so suddenly, especially over what seemed so obviously a setup. Could it be this wasn't the first time Cooper had suspected Ray of sabotaging the *Beauty?*

"Forget about Ray," Cooper muttered as though reading Frank's mind. "He's history."

Cooper reached for a cigarette, then suddenly glanced in his rearview mirror and scowled. Frank looked out the back window. A sleek black Corvette with dark, tinted windows was on their tail, driving dangerously close.

Cooper slammed the accelerator to the floor, throwing the Hardys and Vanessa back against the seat. But the jeep was no match for the Vette. An instant later, the black car was behind them again, driving so close that the bumpers of the two vehicles were practically touching.

"What's with this guy?" Frank wondered out loud.

Joe turned in his seat and read the Vette's vanity license plate. "LYL FLYS. A pilot maybe? The windows are too dark for me to see."

At that moment, the Corvette accelerated and tapped the jeep's rear bumper. Before Cooper could react, the Vette roared up on their left. Then suddenly it veered toward them.

"Watch out!" Joe cried. "He's coming right at us!"

CHAPTER
3

INSTINCTIVELY, Frank reached across the seat and whipped the steering wheel hard to the right. The jeep veered off the road and onto the shoulder, just seconds before the Corvette would have made contact.

Cooper hit the brakes. The jeep bumped over grass and gravel and came to a stop with its front half in a field and its rear half on the shoulder. Back on the road, the driver of the Corvette straightened his course and sped off with a screech toward the airfield.

"When I get my hands on that guy he's going to be dead meat," Cooper said between clenched teeth.

"Who is he?" Joe asked.

"Lyle Freemont," Cooper told him.

"I've seen his photo in the flight annuals," Frank said. "He flies a P-51D Mustang, right?"

"That's him," Cooper said, "and he's as crooked as a broken nose. We flew against each other four years ago. I was in my old plane. It was my last race—until tomorrow, that is."

"What happened?" Vanessa asked.

"Freemont and I were flying neck and neck as we approached the final pylon. A young pilot named Terry Kinert was flying just above us. All of a sudden, Kinert's plane threw a rod and burst into flames. I pulled up five hundred feet, just like the rules say, so Kinert could land. But Freemont—he barely moved."

"I remember reading about that," Frank said. "Freemont came in first, didn't he?"

"You got that right," Cooper said. "Kinert just barely managed to land his plane, and Freemont sailed in for a victory. I took second place. But after the race, I filed a protest with the judges. They saw things my way, and Freemont's first place was overturned." Cooper smiled with satisfaction. "I won the race and Freemont was fined five hundred dollars."

"No wonder he doesn't like you," Joe remarked.

"The feeling is mutual," Cooper shot back, shifting the jeep into gear. "Let's get out of here."

"Mr. Cooper," Frank asked as they drove

21

toward the airfield, "why did you stop racing four years ago?"

Cooper lit a cigarette and inhaled deeply. "I was burned out," he said. "I needed a break. Besides," he added, gazing out the windshield with a furrowed brow, "I've had other things on my mind."

"For example . . ." Joe said.

Cooper turned and scowled at him. "For example, designing *Brett's Beauty*. What else?"

"Nothing else," Joe said as he got out of the jeep. Before shutting the door he asked, "Listen, Mr. Cooper, are you sure you don't want us to check out whether Ray was the one who tampered with the *Beauty?*"

"I already took care of it," Cooper snapped. "I fired Ray. Now, if you'll excuse me, I've got a busted propeller to repair."

As Cooper drove away, Frank turned to Joe and Vanessa. "What a temper! He's like a keg of dynamite about to explode."

"I'll do the same if I don't get something to eat soon," Joe said.

"Let's go to the pilot's clubhouse," Frank suggested. "They've got a coffee shop there that's open to the public."

"And while we're at it," Vanessa added, "let's try to find out who might be trying to sabotage the *Beauty*."

Joe glanced at her. "You heard Mr. Cooper— no snooping."

"True," she replied. "But that's never stopped you before."

Frank nodded. "My thoughts exactly." The trio headed for the clubhouse.

Inside the building, a sign pointed upstairs to the Sky High Coffee Shop. Frank, Joe, and Vanessa climbed the steps and walked in. The restaurant was filled with pilots and pit crew members, boasting loudly about their planes and arguing over who was going to win tomorrow's time trials.

"Check it out," Frank said under his breath. "Some of the most famous airplane race pilots in the world are right here."

Joe nudged Vanessa. "Frank is in aeronautical heaven."

Vanessa and the Hardys grabbed a booth with a good view of the airfield and ordered breakfast. "Hey, there's Bernie Petracca," Frank said, motioning toward a muscular man with a weathered face. "He won at Reno last year. Excuse me, Mr. Petracca," Frank called. "I'm a big fan of yours. How's the Buzzcat running this year?"

"Top notch," Petracca replied. "She's got a new Merlin engine, and I've been doing some work on the wings."

"I hear Brett Cooper's unveiling a new plane this year," Frank said. "Think it's got a chance?"

"Could be," Petracca replied. "Cooper always had good design ideas. Plus, he's a tough competitor.''

"Sure, but he's been off the circuit for four years," one of Petracca's pit crew interrupted. "Who knows if he's still got what it takes?"

"No way of telling until tomorrow," a female crew member said. "Cooper's a lone wolf—always has been. I hear he's been working on this new plane for five years without sponsorship money. The rumor is he's flat broke."

"That's what I heard, too," added a man in a blue jacket. "He'll go bankrupt if he doesn't win this race."

"What's the story with this new plane?" Joe asked innocently. "Has anybody seen it?"

"No, sir," Petracca said. "He's keeping it under wraps until tomorrow." He chuckled. "That's Brett."

"I heard someone found out where his plane is stored and broke in and did some damage," Vanessa said.

"Sabotage?" Petracca asked with interest. "What happened?"

"I don't know the specifics," Vanessa bluffed.

"Maybe it was an inside job," Frank suggested.

"Naw," the man in the blue jacket said. "Cooper's crew is loyal. Especially that dude Kolinsky. He started working for Cooper when he was still in high school. They're like father and son."

Joe glanced at Frank. "They didn't seem like father and son this morning," he said under his breath.

Just then the waitress brought Frank, Joe, and Vanessa their food, and the conversation ended.

"What was all that talk about sponsorship?" Joe asked between mouthfuls of pancake and syrup.

Frank took a sip of his orange juice. "Those planes cost big bucks to maintain," he explained. "Every pilot looks for corporate sponsorship. Take Petracca, for example. He's sponsored by a spark plug company, a beer company, and a gasoline company. In return, Petracca puts their logos on his plane and lets them use his name and his plane in their advertising."

"The only other way to make money in airplane racing is to win races," Vanessa said. "But Uncle Brett hasn't even been doing that."

"No wonder Cooper's so tense," Joe said. "His whole career is riding on the *Beauty*'s success."

Frank took a final bite of toast and glanced out the window. "Look," he said, "there's Lyle Freemont. Let's go talk to him."

Frank, Joe, and Vanessa caught up with Freemont on his way to the ramp. "Mr. Freemont," Frank called as they ran up, "can I have your autograph?"

"Sure, son," the lanky pilot said in a Texas drawl. He opened a leather pouch on his belt and took out a plug of chewing tobacco. "You got a magazine you want me to sign?"

Frank faked an embarrassed laugh. "Boy, that was dumb of me! I left my copy of *Flying* with your photo in the coffee shop."

"That's okay," Lyle said, stuffing the chewing tobacco into his mouth. "I think I've got a publicity photo I can give you. Come with me to the ramp."

"Wow!" Frank exclaimed with a glance at his brother. "Thanks!"

Frank looked around as he followed Freemont across the ramp, a vast, open expanse of blacktop lined with airplanes. The whole area was a flurry of activity as pilots and their pit crews prepared their planes for the next day's time trials.

"They're with me," Freemont said as he walked past a security guard. The guard nodded, and Freemont led the Hardys and Vanessa to his sleek orange and white Mustang, *Wild Child*.

"Think you can beat your old rival, Brett Cooper, tomorrow?" Frank asked as Freemont searched for a photograph in one of the trucks parked beside his plane.

"I don't think it. I *know* it," Freemont shot back.

"Mr. Freemont," Joe lied, "I heard you were robbed in that race four years ago. What really happened?"

"I'll tell you, son," Freemont said, spitting

26

tobacco juice onto the blacktop. "When Kinert's plane burst into flames, I pulled up, just like Cooper did. Only difference was, once I saw Kinert heading for the landing area, I got back on course. Cooper stayed high, so it looked like I was taking advantage of him. But I didn't do anything wrong. Kinert made a safe landing and I won the race."

"The judges didn't see it that way," Vanessa pointed out.

"Yeah?" Freemont snapped, his dark eyes suddenly flashing. "Well, let's see what they say tomorrow when I knock Cooper's precious little plane right out of the sky!"

Just then, Frank noticed something out of the corner of his eye. He looked up to see a hot-pink antique biplane doing a figure eight across the sky. The plane pulled out of the figure eight into a corkscrew, then did three big loops.

By now, Joe, Vanessa, and Freemont were watching the biplane, too. "Boy, that guy can fly!" Joe exclaimed with awe.

At the end of the third loop, the biplane banked and headed toward them. As it came near, the plane stalled and smoke poured out of the wingtips.

"Hey, it looks like something's wrong," Vanessa said nervously.

Suddenly, the nose dipped and the biplane came plummeting toward them.

"Run!" Joe shouted. "It's about to crash!"

Chapter

4

"RELAX!" Lyle Freemont said with a laugh. "That's my girlfriend. She's a top-notch stunt pilot. She'll be putting on a show tomorrow between the time trials."

"You mean, she's not going to crash?" Joe stepped away from the *Wild Child*'s wing, where he'd taken shelter.

"Just watch," Lyle said.

The biplane continued to plummet until it was no more that seventy-five feet over their heads. Then suddenly it pulled up and headed for the clouds. Smoke no longer billowed from the tail. It was flying perfectly normally as it landed a short distance away.

"That woman is an ace pilot," Frank said with admiration. He turned to Lyle Freemont.

"So long, Mr. Freemont. Thanks for the photograph. We're going to go meet your girlfriend."

"Any time, son," Freemont said.

Vanessa and the Hardys jogged up to the biplane just as the pilot was climbing out. She was a pretty, middle-aged woman, small and slender, with wavy blond hair and intelligent blue eyes. She was wearing a hot-pink jumpsuit with the words *Dixie Cooper* emblazoned across the front in curly black letters.

"Dixie Cooper!" Vanessa gasped. "That's Uncle Brett's wife!"

"Hang on," Dixie shouted as she shut down the growling engine. "I can't hear you."

"Mrs. Cooper," Vanessa began, "we never met, but I feel as if I know you. I—"

"That's Ms. Cooper, not Mrs.," Dixie broke in.

"Excuse me," Vanessa said. "I only said Mrs. because I know your husband, Brett Cooper."

Dixie stiffened, and her warm blue eyes suddenly looked like two chips of ice. "Well, you must not know Brett very well. Because if you did, you'd know I only continue to use Cooper as my stage name. In everyday life I'm Dixie Knight. Brett Cooper and I are divorced."

"Divorced!"

"That's right. And next time you see that rat, tell him Lyle Freemont's airplane is going to

29

chew up the *Beauty* and spit her out in little pieces!''

With that, the stunt pilot turned her back on Vanessa and the Hardys and strode off across the airfield.

"Whew! She was *burned!*" Joe exclaimed.

"I don't get it," Vanessa mused. "The last I heard, they were happily married."

"When did they get married?" Frank asked.

"A little over five years ago. Mom went to the wedding, but I was away at camp. Not long after that, Uncle Brett bought the farm in Pennsylvania and went into retirement."

"That means Dixie must know something about the first sabotage attempt on the *Beauty*," Frank said. "In fact, she probably could tell us something about Cooper's change of character."

"I doubt if she wants to talk about it," Joe said. "Did you see the look on her face when you mentioned Brett Cooper? She went into instant attack mode."

"Well, I know someone who will talk to us," Vanessa said. "My mom. Let's go home and see what she knows about all this."

Vanessa and her mother lived in a farmhouse outside of town. Vanessa's father, Harry Bender, had died when Vanessa was an infant. Mrs. Bender was a computer animator with her own studio set up in a converted barn behind the house. The barn had burned down last fall, but

Mrs. Bender had had it rebuilt over the Christmas holidays, and now, Frank noted, it looked as good as new.

Frank, Joe, and Vanessa found Mrs. Bender in her office, working at her computer. "Well, what did you think of *Brett's Beauty?*" she asked.

"Unreal!" Frank exclaimed.

"Mom," Vanessa said, "did you know Uncle Brett and Dixie are divorced?"

"Yes," her mother admitted with a sigh. "Brett didn't tell me himself—you know how private he is—but I heard it from a mutual friend. Apparently, they broke up about six months ago."

"We saw Dixie today," Vanessa said. "When I mentioned Uncle Brett, she acted as if she wanted to rip his head off."

"The gossip around the airfield is that Brett is broke," Frank said, then explained the sabotage attempt on the plane. "Do you know anything about that, Mrs. Bender?"

Mrs. Bender looked baffled. "It seems you know more about Brett Cooper than I do. Maybe I can find out some more tomorrow at the time trials."

"That would be great," Frank said. "Meanwhile, let's go home, Joe. I want to look through my back issues of *Flying* and my *International Air Racing* annuals for articles about Brett Cooper."

31

"I'll see you at the time trials tomorrow," Vanessa said. "Uncle Brett is scheduled to fly his qualifying laps at eleven o'clock."

"Yippee," Joe said. "I can sleep in." He closed his eyes and pretended to snore.

"Save it for later," Frank said, playfully grabbing his brother's nose and silencing him mid-snore. "Right now we've got some investigating to do."

At home, Frank and Joe found their mother and Aunt Gertrude working in the garden. Frank remembered that their father had left for California that morning to investigate a counterfeiting ring.

"Hi, guys," Mrs. Hardy called. She was on her knees among a patch of daffodils, pulling weeds. "How did things go at the airfield?"

"It was an interesting morning," Frank said. "I think we might have uncovered a crime that needs solving."

Quickly, Frank and Joe explained what was going on. "Sounds interesting," Mrs. Hardy said. "What's your next move?"

"Research," Frank told her. "Come on, Joe. Let's check out those articles."

A few minutes later, Frank and Joe were sitting in the kitchen, munching on apples and leafing through Frank's old flying magazines. "Here's a piece about *Brett's Beauty* written four years ago," Frank said, holding up a dog-eared issue of *Flying*. "It tells about Cooper living in Mansfield, Pennsylvania, and working on the plane in his barn. Cooper declined to be interviewed—that sounds like him—but they got some information from one of his crew members."

"Kolinsky?" Joe asked, taking a big bite of his apple.

"No." Frank paused for effect. "Cameron Diller."

"You mean the jerk who buzzed us this morning?" Joe asked with amazement.

"You got it. In the article he talks about Cooper's plans to minimize the frontal area of the aircraft and to use a tail-dragger landing gear to save the weight of a retractable nosewheel."

Frank shook his head. "Considering how secretive Cooper is about the *Beauty,* I'll bet he was furious at Diller for blabbing to the press."

The Hardys' conversation was interrupted by the telephone. "I've got it," Joe said, reaching for the receiver.

"This is Ray Kolinsky," a voice said. "Can I talk to Frank or Joe Hardy?"

"This is Joe," he said, raising his eyebrows at Frank. "What can I do for you?"

"I heard you guys are hotshot detectives." Ray's voice sounded uncertain. "Is that true?"

"We've investigated a number of cases," Joe told him.

"I need your help," Ray blurted, loudly

33

enough to make Joe hold the receiver away from his ear. "I wasn't the one who sabotaged the *Beauty*. But I can't convince Cooper of my innocence unless I find the real bad guy!"

"And you want us to help you find him?" Joe asked.

"You've got to," the voice said desperately. "I've put my whole life into Brett's airplanes. Crewing for anyone else wouldn't be the same."

Joe didn't hesitate. "We'd be glad to help you, Mr. Kolinsky. Can you meet us tomorrow at nine o'clock at the Sky High Coffee Shop?"

"You bet. And please, call me Ray."

"See you tomorrow, Ray."

By the time Joe hung up the phone, he was grinning from ear to ear. "Ray Kolinsky wants us to find out who sabotaged Cooper's plane," he said triumphantly.

Frank jumped to his feet and gave his brother a high five. "All right!" he cried. "The Hardys are on the case!"

"Wake up, Joe," Frank said, shaking his brother out of a sound sleep.

Joe let out a low groan. "What time is it?"

"Six o'clock."

"Six!" Joe moaned. "What's the matter with you? We don't have to meet Ray Kolinsky until nine."

"I know. But this is the perfect time to head out to Cooper's place and do some sleuthing.

Up and at 'em," Frank said. He grabbed the covers and yanked them, exposing Joe's bare chest to the cool morning air.

"Hey!" Joe cried, but Frank was already walking out of the room. Joe grabbed his pillow and threw it, scoring a direct hit to the back of his brother's head. For the first time since waking up, he smiled.

An hour later, the Hardys' van was cruising down the long driveway that led to the Quonset hut where *Brett's Beauty* was stored. The trip had taken a great deal of concentration on Frank and Joe's part because they had been forced to reconstruct the route from memory, based on their one confusing trip to the site the day before. Still, Frank noted with satisfaction, they had only once gotten briefly lost along the way.

Halfway down the driveway, Frank pulled the van off the road and parked. Then the brothers walked the rest of the way to the Quonset hut. Brett's jeep was nowhere in sight.

Joe walked to the doors. "I wish we could take a look inside. Hey," he said suddenly. "Check this out."

The doors were slightly ajar. Joe opened them a little farther and the brothers stepped cautiously inside.

The lights were off. In the gloom, the Hardys could barely make out the *Beauty* sitting in the middle of the room. As their eyes adjusted, they noticed a dozen or more empty soda cans lying on the floor, as well as a variety of tools and greasy airplane parts. The new propeller was in place. Clearly, Brett and his crew had stayed up all night to fix it. From the look of the place, they had only recently left.

Frank and Joe walked slowly toward the plane, stepping over soda cans as they went. Suddenly, they heard a noise, like a chair scraping against cement. They spun around to see a man in gray coveralls and an orange motorcycle helmet hunched over Brett's computer.

"Hey, you!" Joe called.

The man leaped to his feet. He flipped down the plastic visor on his helmet and ran out the doors.

"Get him!" Frank cried, breaking into a run. Joe took off behind him, losing his balance momentarily as he skidded on a patch of grease.

Frank, in the lead, burst through the doors. Suddenly, he felt something hit the back of his head with the force of a jackhammer. Hot, searing pain shot down his neck. He staggered forward, trying to make sense of what was happening. Then he collapsed to the ground.

Chapter
5

"FRANK!" Joe shouted, running outside a second later. He found Frank sprawled on the ground. A man in a plaid shirt was standing over Frank, his back to Joe, with a wrench in his hand.

Joe didn't hesitate. He grabbed the man's shoulder and spun him around, ready to slug him.

"Wait!" the man cried. "It's me—Ray Kolinsky!"

Joe stopped himself mid-slug. "What are you doing here?" he demanded, still clutching Ray's shirt. "And what did you do to my brother?"

At that moment, Frank opened his eyes. "What happened?" he asked groggily.

Joe released Ray and knelt beside his brother. "Are you okay?"

"I'll live," Frank said, sitting up and rubbing the back of his head. He looked up at Ray. "What's going on?"

"I'm really sorry," Ray answered. "I just came by to talk to Brett one more time. I figured once he'd cooled down, he'd probably listen to reason."

"Go on," Joe said.

"As I drove up, I saw a guy in a crash helmet run out of the building. I knew he wasn't one of the crew, so I grabbed a wrench and jumped out of my car. But he had a pretty good head start, so I decided to go inside instead and see if he'd done any damage."

"Then just as you approached the door, I ran out," Frank finished. "So you clocked me."

"You got it," Ray admitted sheepishly. Then he frowned. "What are you guys doing here, anyway? How did you get inside?"

Joe started to answer, but just then a blue and orange dirt bike came roaring around the side of the Quonset hut. The driver was wearing an orange helmet with a darkly tinted plastic visor over his face.

"You stay with Frank," Joe instructed Ray. "I'm going to nail this guy."

Joe ran down the driveway and leaped into the van. He did a quick K-turn and took off after the dirt bike. At the end of the driveway, the cycle turned right, cutting out in front of a dairy truck. Joe was forced to wait for the truck to go by. When he was finally able to make the turn, he was stuck behind the truck going thirty-five miles an hour.

Moments later, the road straightened out. Joe shifted into second and shot past the dairy truck. He shifted again, and soon he was no more than three or four car lengths behind the dirt bike.

The biker glanced over his shoulder. Joe moved up beside the dirt bike, hoping to pressure the rider to pull over. Instead, the man held his ground, and they drove on neck and neck, the dirt bike riding near the shoulder and Joe barreling along halfway over the yellow line.

Suddenly, Joe heard a horn. He looked up to see a large motor home driving toward him on the other side of the road. His heart kicked into overdrive as he hit the brakes and fell back behind the dirt bike, only seconds before the motor home rumbled past him.

Moments later, the dirt bike took a hard right and headed off down a narrow dirt lane. Joe skidded after it, but the Hardys' van was no match for a dirt bike on such rough terrain.

Joe drove on, bumping over rocks and potholes, but soon he caught sight of something that made his heart sink. Up ahead, the path came to an end. As Joe watched in frustration, the dirt bike shot into the woods and disappeared among the trees.

* * *

Back at the Quonset hut, Frank said to Ray, "Let's go inside and check for damage."

They walked back into the hut and Ray flipped on the lights. While he checked out the *Beauty*, Frank looked at the computer and saw that it was on. As Frank sat at the keyboard, he noticed some brown flakes on the keys. He picked some up and sniffed them. Tobacco.

"The *Beauty* looks okay," Ray said, stepping up to join him. "I can't find any obvious damage."

"What do you think about this tobacco?" Frank asked. "Do you suppose it comes from Mr. Cooper's cigarettes?"

"Probably. He usually taps his cigarette against something hard before he lights it."

"Check out the computer," Frank said. "Do you think it's been tampered with?"

Ray sat at the keyboard and typed in some commands. A blueprint of the *Beauty* appeared on the screen. He typed another command, and the computer sequenced through a series of images highlighting various sections of the plane's body, engine, and cockpit.

"It seems to be functioning normally," Ray said. "But I'll have to play around a lot more before I can rest easy."

While Ray continued testing the computer, Frank checked the doors. The lock had been jimmied open with a crowbar. He searched around in the bushes and soon found it.

Just then, Joe drove up in the van and jumped out. "I lost him," he said, with a frustrated expression. "He took off into the woods about three miles up the road."

"I found some evidence," Frank said, holding the crowbar by the curved end and placing it on a towel in the back of the van. "We can check it for prints later."

Frank and Joe went back into the Quonset hut. Ray was still sitting at the computer, running programs. As they walked over to join him, an angry voice boomed out behind them, "What are you three doing here?"

Frank, Joe, and Ray turned around to find Brett Cooper standing in the doorway with a scowl on his face.

"There was a break-in," Ray began. "I came by to talk with you and—"

"There's nothing to talk about," Cooper said. "You're fired, and that's the end of it. And as for you two," he added, addressing the Hardys, "how did you find your way back here?"

"That's not important," Frank said. "What matters is that we found the doors jimmied open and discovered a man tampering with the computer. We chased him, but he got away on a dirt bike."

"How do I know it wasn't you three who were tampering with the computer?" Cooper demanded.

"Mr. Cooper, we're not criminals," Joe said. "You can ask Mrs. Bender if you—"

"I don't have time to ask anyone anything. I've got my qualifying laps to run. Now get out of here before I call the police."

"At least let me check out the computer," Ray said. "If someone messed with the data you could be in serious trouble."

"No, thanks. I'll check it myself."

"Brett, get real," Ray persisted. "I programmed this computer, and I'm the only one who fully understands it."

"That's what I'm worried about," Cooper snapped. "Now get out of here—all three of you."

There was nothing else to say. Frank and Joe led the way, and Ray followed. "We need to talk," Joe said as they stepped outside. "Let's go to the coffee shop and grab some food."

Ray glanced back wistfully at the hut. The gleaming white wing of the *Beauty* was visible through the open doors. "I'll meet you there," he said.

"So you've known Cooper a long time, have you?" Frank asked, digging into his breakfast.

Ray sipped his coffee and nodded. "Since I was fifteen years old. I was an airplane fanatic, always hanging around the airfield back in Indiana, where I grew up. Whenever Brett Cooper came to town, I followed him around like a puppy dog. He was my hero.''

"And eventually you started working for him?'' Joe asked.

"In the beginning I was just a gofer. No pay or anything. Little by little, I learned how to crew. At night I went to school, studying engineering and computer science. Then one year, the day before the finals, the prop pitch control mechanism broke on Brett's Bearcat, and he let me repair it. He went on to place first. When the race ended, he hired me for his crew.''

"You've been with him ever since?'' Frank asked.

"Seven years,'' Ray replied. "When he bought the farm in Pennsylvania and started designing the *Beauty,* I moved there to work with him.''

"Was he married to Dixie then?'' Frank asked.

"They were practically newlyweds,'' Ray said with a smile.

"So what happened?'' Joe asked.

"*That* I wouldn't know,'' Ray said. "Brett and Dixie were like a second mother and father to me, but I don't know what went on behind closed doors.''

"Fair enough,'' Joe said. "How about this one: Why doesn't Cooper have a sponsor?''

Ray laughed. "In case you didn't notice, Brett doesn't like anyone telling him what to do. Be-

43

THE HARDY BOYS CASEFILES

sides, the aircraft companies suspect the *Beauty* has potential beyond Unlimited racing. They want more than just an advertising deal, they want a piece of the plane. Brett won't give up even one percent of the potential profits."

Frank sat back in the booth and stretched out his long legs. "So what's he living on?"

"Hope and a day job," Ray said. "He was flying for a little Pennsylvania airline before he quit to spend more time on the *Beauty*."

"Then why'd he stop racing?" Joe asked.

Ray shrugged. "That's one thing I've never been able to figure out. Brett loves to race. He lives for it. Plus, he needs the prize money—not to mention the sponsorship dollars."

"I thought he didn't like sponsors," Joe said quickly.

"Zable Aviation was the only exception. George Zable is one of Brett's good friends. Anyway, it was only a limited advertising deal. Zable paid a fee and Brett painted Zable Aviation on the side of his F8F-1 Bearcat. No magazine ads or public appearances. Brett didn't go for that sort of thing."

"Was there anything unusual you can think of that happened four years ago, around the time Cooper quit racing?" Frank asked.

Ray frowned thoughtfully. "I don't think so."

"If you come up with anything—anything at all—call us," Joe said.

Ray nodded, and Joe motioned to the waitress for the check.

As she was adding it up, Joe saw the door of the restaurant fly open and a young man in tight jeans, a black T-shirt, and a fringed black leather jacket saunter in. He had shoulder-length blond hair, piercing green eyes, and a chiseled face straight out of a movie magazine. Behind him swarmed a bevy of reporters, vying for his attention.

The young man glanced around the room, then walked straight to the Hardys' booth and stopped in front of Ray. "Beat it, small change," he said coolly. "I need this table for an interview."

Ray's body stiffened. "Think again," he said between clenched teeth. "We're not moving for a cockroach like you."

In the wink of an eye, the man reared back and swung at Ray.

Joe lunged across the table, shouting angrily as he attempted to protect Ray.

But it was too late. The man's fist connected with Ray's cheek, sending him flying out of the booth and crashing to the floor.

Chapter
6

AS RAY hit the floor, the man with the long blond hair jumped on him. Ray managed a quick jab to his opponent's jaw. The man returned a searing punch to Ray's stomach.

"Break it up!" Joe ordered, grabbing the blond man by the back of his leather jacket and dragging him off Ray.

"Get lost, creep!" the man shouted, taking a swing at Joe.

Joe ducked, then connected with a solid right to the man's mouth. The man fell back, flailing his arms in a desperate attempt to regain his balance.

Frank was there to catch him as he fell. He grabbed the man's arms and pinned them behind his back.

"Hey, let me go!" the man yelled, struggling hard. But Frank held him tight.

Meanwhile, Ray had scrambled to his feet. Now he stepped up to the man, his face only inches from the handsome profile, and said, "How do you feel now, Diller? Not so tough, huh?"

"This is Cameron Diller?" Frank asked in surprise.

"The moron who buzzed us yesterday morning!" Joe cried.

"Was that you?" Diller said with a smirk. "Pleased to meet you, gentlemen."

"You could kill someone that way," Joe said angrily. "All it takes is one mistake."

"I don't make mistakes," Diller shot back. He smiled a toothy shark grin. "How about letting me go, guys? You're ruining my jacket. Besides, I've got an interview to do."

Frank and Joe had been concentrating so hard on breaking up the fight that they had forgotten everything else. Now they looked around and realized that everyone in the restaurant was staring at them.

Frank released Diller. Ignoring the booth where Ray and the Hardys had been sitting, the pilot sauntered over to an empty booth and sat down. Immediately, he was surrounded by reporters.

"I'm out of here," Ray said. "This guy makes me sick."

47

"I think you might want to stick around," Frank replied. "I'm going to push a few of Diller's buttons and see what happens."

Reluctantly, Ray did as he was asked. He and the Hardys stood at the back of the crowd of reporters, listening to the questions they threw at Diller.

"What's your strategy for the race, Cameron?" a reporter asked.

"Who needs strategy when you've got the *Killer Diller?*" Diller replied. "The engine is wound so tight, all I have to do is blow on the throttle and she takes off."

"Think you've got the stuff to beat Brett Cooper's new plane?" someone else asked.

"That flying hunk of aluminum foil?" Diller scoffed. "I used to work for Cooper, man. In fact, I'm the only rival pilot who's actually seen any of his blueprints." He laughed. "That plane is dirt. Pure garbage."

Frank stepped forward. "Excuse me, Mr. Diller," he said loudly. "I'm a reporter for the Bayport High School newspaper. Do you mind if I ask a question?"

"You?" Diller chuckled. "Fire away."

"Why did you stop working for Brett Cooper?"

Diller shrugged. "I learned all he could teach me in about a month. It was time to move on."

"That's not true," Ray broke in. "You were fired and you know it! Brett asked you to keep the details of his new plane secret, but you talked to *Flying* magazine.''

"Big deal," Diller muttered testily.

"What about that break-in at Cooper's farm a few years ago?" Frank asked. "I read that the *Beauty* was damaged with a sledgehammer. Did you work for Cooper then?''

"Why don't you ask Kolinsky about that?" Diller said. "He's the one who was using a sledgehammer." He looked at Ray. "Remember that old shed you were knocking down behind the barn? That *was* a sledgehammer you used, wasn't it?''

"Shut up!" Ray shouted furiously. "You don't know the meaning of the word loyalty!''

Diller grinned. "Maybe not. But I know what revenge means. And that's exactly what I'm going to get when I leave Brett Cooper's pathetic little toy plane in the dust.'' Diller stood up and pushed his way through the cluster of reporters. "The interview is over, gentlemen. See you on the runway.''

The restaurant emptied out quickly. Frank, Joe, and Ray followed the reporters out of the clubhouse and into the parking lot. "It sounds as if Diller still hasn't forgiven Brett Cooper for firing him," Joe said.

"He's just a loudmouth kid with something to prove," Ray said sullenly.

"You think he's the one who's been sabotaging the *Beauty?*" Frank asked.

"I wouldn't put it past him," Ray said.

Joe looked Ray straight in the eye. "Sounds as if he wouldn't put it past you."

Ray froze in his tracks. "I didn't do it!" he said passionately. "My fingerprints were on the sledge-hammer, but so what?" Ray glared at the Hardys, then strode off toward his car.

Frank and Joe looked at each other as Ray drove away in his Honda. "The list of suspects keeps growing," Joe said.

Frank nodded. "Cameron Diller, Lyle Free-mont, Ray Kolinsky. Got any hunches?"

"Only one," Joe replied. "This is going to be a tough case to crack."

"We'd better hurry," Frank said, walking across the airfield with Joe, Vanessa, and Mrs. Bender later that morning. "Brett Cooper's quali-fying race starts in twenty minutes."

Though his brother was the airplane fan, Joe had to admit the crowded airfield and the roar of modified World War II fighter planes were enough to excite anyone. He glanced up at the cloudless blue sky. Dixie was putting on a show for the crowd—pulling off loops, rolls, corkscrews, and a few maneuvers Joe couldn't name. Each time she did a trick, the people in the stands let out a whoop and waved their programs.

"Where are we sitting?" Joe asked.

"Section three, of course," Vanessa said. She pointed to a bleacher section filled with rowdy, cheering men and women in orange T-shirts.

"The section three gang formed almost ten years ago at the Reno Air Races," Mrs. Bender explained. "People who came to the races every year began to recognize each other. Eventually, section three evolved into a full-fledged fraternity with its own colors and scrapbook."

"Some of the members even travel cross-country together, hitting all the air shows," Vanessa added.

"And your mom's part of the section three gang?" Frank asked eagerly.

Instead of answering, Mrs. Bender unzipped her windbreaker to reveal an orange T-shirt. Then she reached into her handbag and pulled out two more. "Now you're honorary members," she said, handing them to Frank and Joe.

"All right!" the brothers exclaimed together. They slipped on their T-shirts and followed the Benders into the stands. Soon Mrs. Bender was chatting happily with her old friends.

Dixie's biplane did one more series of loops and landed on the runway. Then she taxied past the grandstand and revved the engine with the brakes locked, compressing the nose gear strut to take a bow. The crowd went wild.

"That was Dixie Cooper, ladies and gentlemen!" the announcer boomed over the loudspeakers. "Let's give her a hand. And now," he continued when the applause had died down, "it's time for the time trials."

"How do the time trials work?" Joe asked Mrs. Bender.

"There are eight pylons, each forty feet high, arranged in an irregular rectangle," she answered. "The course is just over nine miles. In the time trials, each plane flies alone twice around the course. During the actual race, the planes fly together eight times around."

"It sounds like a long race," Vanessa added, "but it's not. The pilots cover seventy-two miles at almost five hundred miles per hour. It's over in about ten minutes!"

The announcer's booming voice broke into their conversation. "The next pilot to fly will be Lyle Freemont in his orange and white P-51D Mustang, *Wild Child.*"

Freemont taxied past the grandstand and headed down the runway for takeoff.

"He's up," the announcer said as the *Wild Child* lifted off and headed for the course.

The first pylon was less than three hundred yards away from the grandstands. Joe could feel his chest vibrate as the powerful Mustang roared by.

Freemont flew twice around the course. Then the plane's wings tipped up and down. "Okay, folks, he's waggling his wings," the announcer said. "That means he's ready to be timed. Go for it, Lyle!"

Joe watched in awe as the nose dipped and the *Wild Child* took off at top speed, flying no more than fifty feet above the ground. Freemont thundered around the pylons, edging as close as possible without cutting inside. The crackle of supersonic shocks generated by the propeller tips rang through the air.

After his second pass, Freemont pulled up and circled back to the landing strip. There was a suspense-filled pause as the judges calculated his time.

"Four hundred and seventy-seven miles per hour!" the announcer exclaimed. The crowd let out a cheer.

"That's good flying," Mrs. Bender said. "He'll qualify easily."

Frank and Joe watched as the *Wild Child* landed. Dixie Cooper ran over to meet Lyle Freemont as he taxied into the pit. With her was a well-dressed man, about sixty, with thinning white hair. His suit and tie looked out of place on the ramp. Dixie hugged Freemont as he emerged from the plane, and the distinguished man shook his hand.

"And now, ladies and gentlemen," the announcer said, "from Bakersfield, California, let's welcome our next pilot, Cameron Diller!"

At the mere mention of Diller's name, a group of girls in the front rows cheered and whistled.

"He's got quite a fan club," Frank said.

"No surprise," Vanessa replied as Diller taxied past the stands and took a bow. "He's handsome!"

Joe shot her a withering look. "He's the guy who buzzed us yesterday morning."

Vanessa's appreciative smile turned to a frown. "Oh. Well, he may have the looks, but he's obviously missing a few brain cells."

"There he goes," Joe heard the announcer say as Diller took off. "Cameron Diller tells us he's made some recent modifications to the *Killer Diller* that will really improve her speed. Let's see if he's right."

The Bearcat did three test runs around the course, then Diller waggled the wings.

"Look at him go, folks!" the announcer cried. "He's really moving!"

The *Killer Diller* blasted around the course for all she was worth. Joe leaned forward in his seat, waiting for the results.

"Hey, look at that!" the announcer suddenly exclaimed.

Joe looked around. It was *Brett's Beauty*, flying in from the opposite direction of the course. Its sleek white body gleamed like a diamond in the sunlight. The crowd let out a gasp as the *Beauty* came in for a landing and taxied in front of the grandstands.

"It's Brett Cooper," the announcer said, "unveiling his brand-new Unlimited racer, *Brett's Beauty!* As you might have heard, Brett has been keeping his new plane a secret for five years, until this very moment. And isn't she something, folks? Bet you've never seen an Unlimited that looks like that!"

The crowd was buzzing with excitement. No one was paying any attention to Cameron Diller, despite the fact that he had finished his qualifying laps and was coming in for a landing.

"The *Killer Diller* just ran the course at four hundred and eighty-one miles per hour," the announcer said. "That's a new qualifying record!"

But no one seemed to hear, because Brett Cooper had just lifted the canopy of the *Beauty* and was waving to the crowd. Everyone in the grandstands burst into wild applause.

"And now it's time for Brett Cooper's qualifying laps," the announcer said as Cooper closed the canopy and readied his plane for takeoff. "There he goes, folks! Now we'll see what this baby can do!"

Joe watched as the *Beauty* flew gracefully past the first pylon. After three laps, Cooper waggled the wings, and the judges started their stopwatches. The *Beauty* thundered around the course, rejecting the tight, steeply banked turns used by the fighter planes in favor of wider, smoother ones.

"She's really moving, folks!" the announcer cried. "I think we might have a new qualifying record here!"

The *Beauty* finished her initial lap and roared around the first pylon to begin lap two. Suddenly, as she passed the second pylon, the engines sputtered.

The crowd let out a collective gasp. The *Beauty* choked and sputtered for another second, then the engines died.

"Uncle Brett's going to crash!" Vanessa cried.

Frank and Joe leaped to their feet, but there was nothing they could do. As they watched helplessly, the *Beauty*'s nose tipped forward and the plane began to fall.

Chapter

7

FRANK STARED in horror as the *Beauty* plummeted toward the earth. In another instant, he knew, it would crash. Then without warning, the engines kicked in again.

The *Beauty* was only twenty feet from the ground when it pulled out of its nosedive and straightened out. Frank watched, his heart in his throat, as the plane roared over the ramp, a mere thirty feet above the other planes, before it finally began to rise again.

"Looks like Cooper's going to be all right!" the announcer told the crowd. "He's turning back to finish his last lap."

"Thank goodness!" Mrs. Bender exclaimed.

Joe squeezed Vanessa's hand. Frank took a long, slow breath and glanced toward the ramp to check the other pilots' reactions to Cooper's near-disaster. To his surprise, he noticed Dixie staring up at her ex-husband's plane with a hand over her mouth and tears in her eyes. She didn't relax until the *Beauty* finished its final lap and headed in for a landing.

"Hang on to your hats, folks," the announcer said. "The *Beauty* flew that first lap at four hundred eighty-five miles per hour! That's a new qualifying speed record!" The crowd let out a roar of approval.

Mrs. Bender was on her feet and heading down the aisle. "I'm going to find out what happened," she said to Vanessa and the Hardys. "You want to come along? I have a pit pass."

Frank, Joe, and Vanessa followed Mrs. Bender out of the grandstands, past the guards, and onto the ramp. Then they jogged to the far end, where the *Beauty* was just taxiing in from the runway.

The *Beauty* rolled into the pit and came to a stop. Cooper killed the engines and threw open the canopy.

"Brett, are you all right?" Mrs. Bender called anxiously.

Cooper's face was pale and pasty. "That was a close one," he said in a husky voice.

"What was the problem, Mr. Cooper?" Frank asked.

"I don't know," Cooper said, climbing out.

"The plane was flying like a dream and then *pffft*—nothing."

"What about when she turned back on?" Joe asked.

"Same thing. One second she was falling, the next second it was all systems go."

"It must have been caused by a command buried in one of the computer programs," Frank said. "Probably introduced into the system by that guy we caught snooping around the Quonset hut."

"Or Ray Kolinsky," Cooper reminded them.

"Either way, this is serious," Mrs. Bender said. "You could have been killed."

Cooper nodded. For the first time since the Hardys had met him, he looked truly shaken. "It's not just me I'm worried about," he said soberly. "Innocent bystanders could have been hurt. I can't take a chance of something like that happening again."

"That's why you need to let Joe and Frank investigate, Uncle Brett," Vanessa urged. "They can help you find out who's behind this."

"I can vouch for them," Mrs. Bender said. "Frank and Joe have a track record even the police department would envy."

Cooper looked Frank and Joe up and down. "If Andrea says you're okay," he said at last, "then I guess you are." He shrugged. "Go for it."

Frank smiled. "The first thing we need to do

is check out your computer and see what went wrong.''

"I have an idea," Joe said, "Tell your pit crew you've hired us to help out. That way we'll have an excuse to hang around the *Beauty* and keep an eye on—"

"Mr. Cooper!" Mr. Cooper!" a confusion of voices called.

The Hardys looked up to see a dozen or more reporters approaching the pit, pencils poised over their notepads.

"Here come the barracudas," Cooper said dryly. He turned to Mrs. Bender. "Andrea, introduce Frank and Joe to the crew, will you?"

While Cooper went off to be interviewed about his record-breaking qualifying laps, Mrs. Bender led the Hardys over to the pit crew. Frank recognized the two men who had watched from their trailer as Cooper fired Ray Kolinsky the day before.

"Hi, Stan. Hi, Jesse. That's some plane your boss designed," Mrs. Bender said.

"Long time no see," Stan said, shaking Mrs. Bender's hand warmly with his pale, freckled one.

"Still hanging with the section three crowd, I see," added Jesse, the barrel-chested crew member.

"You bet," Mrs. Bender told him. "Guys, I want you to meet the newest addition to the

Beauty's crew. Brett just hired them—Frank Hardy and his brother, Joe."

"Right. I saw you at the Quonset hut when Ray was fired," Jesse remarked. "Were you hired to replace him?"

"I guess you could say that," Frank said. "Mr. Cooper wants me to check out the computer system and see what went wrong."

"No problem," Stan replied. He waved to Mrs. Bender and Vanessa as they went off to watch the rest of the time trials. "I'll hook up the computer terminal to the *Beauty*'s on-board computer."

"What about you?" Jesse asked Joe.

Joe hesitated. He didn't know very much about airplanes, compared to Frank, at least. "I'm just an apprentice," he said at last. "I'll do whatever odd jobs you need done."

Jesse smiled mischievously. "We've got a special job reserved for rookies. Follow me." While Frank followed Stan into the motor home that housed the computer terminal, Jesse led Joe to the *Beauty* and handed him a stack of clean white rags and a five-pound box of cornstarch.

"What am I supposed to do with these?" Joe asked.

"Even a few spots of dirt can nibble away precious airspeed," Jesse said. "So start polishing."

"The whole plane?" Joe asked incredulously. "By hand?"

"For starters," Jesse replied with a grin. "Then you can go over it again with an electric buffer."

With a sigh, Joe set to work.

Inside the motor home, Frank was learning his way around the sophisticated computer programs that Ray had designed to operate the *Beauty*. Stan knew enough to show him the basics. After that, he was on his own.

First, Frank ran the safety programs that were designed to check each system and identify any malfunctioning equipment. Ray had already run them earlier that morning after they'd found the helmeted intruder in the Quonset hut, but Frank figured it wouldn't hurt to go through them again. Everything checked out fine, so he moved on to the telemetry programs that monitored the airplane in mid-flight.

All the instrumentation templates seemed intact, and so did the hydraulics oversight program. For one heart-stopping second he thought he had found a bug when he got an error message in the altimeter adjustment program, but then he realized it was his own fault.

Half an hour later, Frank took a break from the keyboard. On the tiny kitchen table he noticed a leather briefcase and a stack of bills. There were two overdue credit-card bills totaling almost $20,000, rental bills for the Quonset hut and the motor home, and a $50,000 bill from Zable

Aviation for various engine parts. There was also a letter from a collection agency for dozens of bills Cooper had left unpaid back in Pennsylvania.

Wow, Frank thought, those crew guys we talked to at the coffee shop weren't kidding when they said Brett Cooper was in debt!

Frank glanced over the Zable Aviation invoice. Cooper had ordered a speed-reduction gearbox last winter, and another in the spring. He had also ordered three turbochargers in a six-month period.

Was it normal for the *Beauty* to break down that often? Frank wondered, returning to the computer keyboard. Or had the plane been sabotaged even more times than Cooper had admitted?

Frank was still running programs when Brett Cooper finally showed up.

"I hate reporters," the airman growled, lighting a cigarette. "They're like ambulance chasers. More interested in the fact that I almost crashed than in my new speed record."

"Speaking of your near-crash," Frank said, "I think I might be onto something. Look at this."

Frank turned back to the terminal and punched one of the function keys. The screen cleared, and then a string of commands appeared. "It took me a while," he said, "but I dug this up in a hidden sector of your hard disk." He pointed to a mid-screen sequence.

"Does that say what I think it does?" Cooper asked.

"Yes. The first time your engine hits four thousand rpm's after running for at least two minutes at an altitude of fifty feet or more, the computer shuts it down for ten seconds, then turns it on again."

"But that's crazy!" Cooper fumed. "If someone wanted to destroy the *Beauty,* why wouldn't they program her to hit four thousand rpm's and shut down completely? Why just ten seconds?"

"Maybe the goal wasn't to make you crash," Frank suggested. "Maybe someone just wanted to scare you."

"Well, they succeeded," Cooper snapped. "But what's the point?"

Frank tapped a key on the keyboard and the screen went blank. "That's what we have to find out."

"This is a new recipe I got from one of my bridge partners," Aunt Gertrude said at dinner that evening. "It's a traditional Sicilian tomato sauce."

After a long afternoon polishing the *Beauty,* Joe felt certain he could eat all the spaghetti in Sicily. But when he grabbed his fork and dug in, he found his hands were so stiff he could barely twirl the pasta. He clutched his fork tighter. Droplets of sauce splattered across the table.

Aunt Gertrude clucked her tongue. "Joe, watch your manners."

Joe was about to apologize when the phone rang. He grabbed a piece of garlic bread on his way to the kitchen. "Hello?" he said into the phone.

"Hi, Joe. This is Vanessa."

"Just the person I need to dispense some sympathy," Joe said. "Working for Cooper is like joining a chain gang."

"Important news first, sympathy later," Vanessa broke in.

"What is it?" Joe said, suddenly on the alert.

"My mom's brother has been Uncle Brett's insurance agent for years. Tonight Mom was talking to him on the phone, and guess what she found out? Brett owns a five hundred thousand dollar insurance policy."

"What's so unusual about that? He's in a pretty dangerous profession."

"It's not the policy that's unusual. It's the beneficiary. If Uncle Brett dies, all the money goes to Dixie Cooper."

"So that means . . ." Joe began.

"Right," Vanessa finished. "Dixie might be trying to kill Uncle Brett to cash in on the money."

Chapter

8

"LET'S GO OVER this again," Vanessa said. "What exactly do you want me to say to Dixie?"

It was early the next morning, and Joe and Vanessa were driving to the airfield in Vanessa's car.

"Just tell her you're interested in stunt flying and you want to pick her brain," Joe answered. "Anything to get her relaxed and talking."

"And then what?" Vanessa said with a wry smile. "Ask her if she tried to murder Uncle Brett?"

Joe rolled his eyes. "Try being a little more subtle. See if you can find out what she knows about the insurance. Try to get a sense of how she feels about Cooper."

"She acted like she hated him last time," Vanessa remarked.

"Yes, but when Cooper almost crashed, Dixie had tears in her eyes. That's not how someone who hates him would act."

Now that Joe was working on Cooper's crew, he had only to flash his pit pass to gain access to the ramp.

"This shouldn't be too tough to fake," Vanessa said as they searched the ramp for Dixie's hot-pink biplane. "I really do think stunt flying is thrilling. I'd love to try it."

"There she is," Joe said, pointing to Dixie. The stunt pilot was standing on the wing of her plane, checking the timing of the spark plugs.

"Excuse me, Ms. Cooper," Vanessa called. "I mean, Ms. Knight."

Dixie turned around with a smile on her face. But when she saw Joe and Vanessa, her smile turned to a frown. "You again? Did you deliver my message to Brett Cooper?"

Dixie's eyes were cold as ice, but Vanessa wasn't intimidated. "Ms. Knight," she said, "I didn't come up to you the other day to argue with you. I just wanted to tell you how impressed I am with your flying." She paused. "You see, I've always dreamed of becoming a stunt pilot someday and . . . well, I was wondering if you could give me some tips."

Dixie's frown wavered. "Do you have your

pilot's license?'' she asked, hopping off the wing and putting down her timing gun.

"Not yet," Vanessa bluffed. "But, uh . . . Joe's brother is giving me lessons."

"What's your name, honey?" Dixie asked.

"Vanessa."

"Well, Vanessa, I'm about to take this baby up for a test run." She patted the fuselage of her plane. "If you promise you won't mention that ex-husband of mine, I might take you along."

"I promise," Vanessa said eagerly.

Dixie reached into her pocket and pulled out a pair of goggles. "Put these on, honey. You and I are going for a ride."

While Joe and Vanessa were at the airfield, Frank took care of some unfinished business. First, he called the Mansfield, Pennsylvania, police department and asked for the chief.

"This is Frank Hardy in Bayport, New York," he said. "I'm calling on behalf of my father, Fenton Hardy."

"Fenton Hardy?" the chief repeated. "You mean the private eye?"

"That's him," Frank replied. "We're doing research on a possible sabotage attempt. Could you check your records and tell me if you ever got a call to investigate a break in at a farm owned by Brett Cooper?"

"There has never been any official report of

a break-in," the chief replied after checking a computer. "But between you and me, Coop's crew chief, Ray Kolinsky, did ask me to do a little investigating."

"Did you ever uncover anything?" Frank asked.

"Nothing. One time we thought we had a lead—Coop's plane was damaged with a sledgehammer, and we found one with Kolinsky's prints on it. But Coop confirmed that Kolinsky had been using the sledgehammer with his knowledge the day before, so that didn't help us."

Frank let out a disappointed sigh. "Thanks for your help," he said.

Next, Frank took the crowbar he had found outside Cooper's Quonset hut to the Bayport police.

"Why didn't you bring this to us right away?" Officer Con Riley asked when he saw the crowbar. Riley had helped the Hardys with their investigations many times. He was a seasoned veteran with a reputation for doing things by the book. "And why wasn't this break-in reported to the police?"

"Sorry, but things have been kind of hectic," Frank answered. "Anyway, I'm reporting it now."

Riley rolled his eyes. "Okay, okay. I'll send this to the lab and call you later with the results. And, Frank, I know it's pointless to ask you and

Joe to stay out of this. But please, try not to get yourselves into hot water."

Frank smiled. "I'll call you if things start to boil over."

While Vanessa was flying with Dixie, Joe decided to see what was happening with the *Beauty*. He found Brett Cooper cleaning the engines' cylinder heads while a couple of dozen racing fans with pit passes stood behind a barrier watching.

"Hey, Mr. Cooper," Joe called. "Can I help?"

Cooper nodded, and Joe joined him. "Well," Cooper asked, "did you find out who messed with the *Beauty*'s computer?"

Joe laughed. "Not quite yet."

But Cooper was serious. "Why not?"

"Mr. Cooper, it's been less than twenty-four hours since you asked us to investigate. Be patient."

"I can't afford to be," he snapped. "I'm flying in my heat race tomorrow morning. I need to be sure the *Beauty* hasn't been tampered with."

"Look, we're doing our best," Joe said, his temper rising. "In fact, right this minute my girlfriend is questioning your ex-wife to find out if she might be the culprit."

"Dixie?" Cooper said incredulously. "Don't make me laugh. She wouldn't have the guts to pull off something like that."

"You don't sound as if you like her very much."

"Like her?" Cooper growled. "I *hate* her!"

"Then why is it you have a five hundred thousand dollar insurance policy that names her as beneficiary?"

"What?" Cooper cried. "How did you find out about that?"

Joe smiled. "It's called investigation. It's what you asked us to do, remember?"

"Yes. Yes, of course." Cooper took a deep breath and made a visible effort to calm himself. "Look, I've been planning to take Dixie's name off that policy. I've just been too busy. But trust me, Dixie isn't behind the sabotage attempts."

"How can you be so sure?" Joe asked.

"I just am!" Cooper almost shouted. Then he added, "Listen, son, could you go to the clubhouse and see if the heat schedule has been posted yet?"

As Joe walked to the clubhouse, he thought about his conversation with Cooper. The pilot's claim that he hadn't had time to take Dixie off his insurance policy seemed pretty lame. If his feelings weren't quite what they seemed, what was the point of lying?

Joe checked the heat schedule and headed back to the pit. "Hey, Joe, wait up!" a voice called.

Joe turned to see Frank jogging toward him.

Quickly, the two exchanged the information they had recently uncovered.

"What now?" Joe asked.

"I'm heading over to the pit," Frank said. "Mr. Cooper and I are going to reprogram the computer this afternoon and double-check all the systems. What about you?"

"Tell Cooper he's flying in the eight o'clock heat tomorrow morning. I'll wait for Vanessa," he replied. "I want to see if she learned anything from Dixie."

"While you're waiting, ask around about Ray Kolinsky," Frank suggested. "We haven't seen or heard from him since he had that fight with Cameron Diller in the coffee shop. I've been wondering what became of him."

"Good idea. I'll catch you later."

Joe spent the next hour in the coffee shop, chatting with the pilots and crew members. None of them had seen or heard from Ray since before the time trials. Eventually, Joe saw Vanessa walking toward the parking lot. He hurried out to meet her.

"Hi!" he called. "How was it?"

Vanessa's long hair was windblown and her blue-gray eyes were shining. "Incredible!" she cried. "Dixie took me through all her tricks—corkscrews, loops, Cuban eights, stalls. It was a total blast!"

"Did you ask her about Cooper?"

Vanessa nodded. "After we landed, we sat

around and talked for a while. Dixie was in such a good mood, I managed to slip in a few questions about Uncle Brett. If you ask me, she doesn't hate him. It's just that she was really hurt by him."

"What do you mean?" Joe asked.

"It started after Uncle Brett quit racing," she explained. "He became moody and temperamental. He snapped at her over every little thing. Then he started smoking and gambling. Finally, she couldn't take it anymore, and she left him."

"Did you ask her why Cooper quit racing?"

"Yes, but she doesn't know. He never explained why, and whenever she suggested he start racing again, he flew into a rage."

Joe gave Vanessa a kiss on the cheek. "Good sleuthing, Nessa. Next time you talk to Dixie, ask her if she can remember anything significant that happened just before Cooper quit racing."

"I'll ask her after the heats tomorrow," Vanessa said with enthusiasm. "Dixie is taking me up again, and this time she's going to start teaching me how to work the controls."

Back in the motor home, Frank and Cooper were running programs on the computer when the door opened and a man walked in. Frank recognized him as the well-dressed man who had accompanied Dixie to Lyle's plane after his qualifying laps.

"Howdy, Brett," he said. "Hope I'm not interrupting anything."

"Come on in," Brett replied. "George, this is Frank Hardy. He's replacing Kolinsky on the crew. Frank, this is my former sponsor, George Zable."

As they shook hands, Frank took a closer look at Zable. He was in his early sixties, with thinning white hair.

"Mr. Zable," Frank said, "I learned recently that your company used to sponsor Mr. Cooper."

"That was long ago and far away," Zable said fondly, taking a seat at the kitchen table. "Back when Brett was flying his old Bearcat."

"Forget the Bearcat, George," Cooper interrupted. "Did you see my qualifying laps? Four hundred and eighty-five miles per hour! And those engines still had more to give."

"You looked good, Brett. But you still have to prove the *Beauty* has what it takes to run eight laps against the big boys."

"Just watch me!"

Zable's face grew suddenly serious. "How's your money holding out?"

Copper shrugged. "I'm getting by."

"My offer still holds," Zable said. "If you let me sponsor you, you'll get all the money you need, plus a generous salary. All I ask in return is a small percentage of whatever you make off the *Beauty*."

Cooper hesitated.

"Don't answer me now," Zable added quickly. "Wait until after the heats tomorrow. Then we'll both know a little better what the *Beauty* can do." He stood up and reached into his pocket. "In the meantime, take care of yourself," he added, quietly putting a hundred dollar bill on the table.

"George, I can't—"

"Take it. What are friends for?"

"Hey," Cooper said suddenly, "I was just about to take the *Beauty* up for a test run. You want to come along, George?"

"I'd love to, but I've got an appointment. I'll watch you take off."

"Can I come with you, Mr. Cooper?" Frank asked eagerly.

"Sure, son. Up, up, and away!"

Fifteen minutes later, Frank was wedged into the tiny two-seat cockpit next to Cooper as the *Beauty* soared through the clouds. Below them, farms and fields flew by at breakneck speed.

Frank glanced at the airspeed indicator. Four hundred miles per hour!

"When you're moving this fast," Cooper shouted over the growl of the engines, "you can't lose your concentration for an instant. In the time it takes to sneeze, you could slam into a mountain."

Frank silently prayed Cooper didn't have hay fever.

"Check this out," Cooper said. "I'm going to bank hard and pull G."

He hit the throttle and used the stick to manipulate the wing flaps. The *Beauty* banked ninety degrees to the left. Frank could feel his body press hard against the seat as the G forces kicked in.

Frank's heart was pounding with exhilaration. He glanced out the window at the *Beauty*'s shadow moving across the landscape. Then suddenly, he noticed another shadow directly behind it. He craned his neck to look out the rear of the cockpit. Cameron Diller's red and black Bearcat was flying only a few hundred feet behind them.

"Mr. Cooper, look," Frank said, pointing. "The *Killer Diller* is on our tail."

Cooper grinned. "Let's see if that little punk can keep up with us."

But before Cooper could hit the throttle, the *Killer Diller* accelerated hard and overtook them. With an ear-splitting roar, the Bearcat flew over them, so close that the *Beauty* was caught in the corkscrewing wind created by the propellers.

Trapped in the *Killer Diller*'s prop wash, the *Beauty* was tossed upside down. Frank and Cooper were thrown forward in their seats.

Frank's helmet slammed against the controls, cracking the glass on the altimeter. Quickly, he sat up and turned to Cooper, who was still slumped over the controls.

Frank grabbed the pilot's shoulder and pulled him upright. Blood streamed from Cooper's nose. "Mr. Cooper, are you all right?" Frank cried.

But Cooper couldn't answer. He was out cold.

JOE AND VANESSA had been sitting in the Sky
High Coffee Shop when Frank and Cooper had
taken off in the *Beauty*. From where they were
sitting, they had a perfect view of the plane's
flight—and its unexpected descent.

"Uncle Brett!" Vanessa gasped as the *Beauty*
began to plummet.

"He's probably just hotdogging to show
Diller up," Joe said, not knowing his brother
was also in the plane. "Isn't that Diller's
plane above there?" But the *Beauty* just kept
plunging down, showing no sign of gaining
altitude.

"Cooper's in trouble," Joe said, his chest
growing tight.

"Diller must have hedge-hopped Uncle Brett,

and now the *Beauty*'s out of control," Vanessa said angrily.

"Hedge-hopped? What's that?"

"Diller flew so close that the *Beauty* was caught in the *Killer Diller*'s prop wash—the wind from the propellers."

"So how does Cooper regain control?" Joe asked.

"He doesn't," Vanessa said tightly.

"We've got to do something!" Joe shouted.

He threw some money down on the table, raced toward the door, and shouted to the man behind the cash register, "Call nine one one! Cooper's airplane is about to crash in the fields about three miles northeast of here."

The *Beauty* was falling fast. Glancing nervously out of the canopy, Frank saw sky below him. Where the sky was supposed to be, he saw the ground moving up to meet him.

"Oh, no," Frank said, sucking in his breath. "I'm too young to die."

There was no time to wait for Cooper to regain consciousness. Frank knew he had to act immediately, or they would both be killed.

Frank leaned across Cooper's limp body and grabbed the joystick. He pushed the pilot's legs aside and placed his feet on the rudder controls. Leg muscles straining, he worked the foot pedals, forcing the rudders and ailerons into position.

"Come on, *Beauty*, you can do it," Frank pleaded.

The plane responded, flipping upright. But the nose was still pointing downward. The *Beauty* was heading for a clump of trees at breakneck speed. There was no time to regain altitude. The best Frank could hope for was a safe landing.

Frank yanked the joystick toward him. At the same time, he released the landing gear. The *Beauty* leveled out, grazing the tops of the trees. There was a loud *crack* as the branches made contact with the landing gear.

The *Beauty* reeled from the impact, but Frank managed to keep her on course. On the other side of the trees, a newly plowed field stretched out before him.

"Okay, *Beauty*, do your thing," Frank said desperately.

Frank brought the plane down in the dirt. The impact threw him out of his seat. He felt his helmet whack against the top of the canopy. Beside him, Cooper's limp body did the same.

The *Beauty* bumped and skidded across the field and finally shuddered to a halt. Frank threw open the canopy and leaped up, sucking the cool air into his lungs. "Yes!" he exclaimed. "I did it!"

"Ooh," a weak voice moaned. "What happened?"

Frank looked down to see Cooper's eyes fluttering open.

"Mr. Cooper," Frank said hesitantly, "I don't know how to tell you this, but, uh . . . we didn't quite make it back to the airport."

Back at the airfield, Joe and Vanessa ran out of the coffee shop and into the parking lot. Just as they were getting into Vanessa's car, Joe noticed Cameron Diller driving up.

Joe nudged Vanessa. "Am I seeing things?"

"Diller!" she cried. "But he's up in his plane!"

"Apparently not. Come on."

Joe and Vanessa intercepted the pilot. "Diller," Joe said, "someone's up in your plane."

"Oh, sure," the young hotshot said. "Tell me another one."

"We're serious," Vanessa insisted. "The *Killer Diller* just hedge-hopped my Uncle Brett's plane."

"What?" Diller cried. "Are you crazy? No one flies the *Killer Diller* except me. Anyhow, I've been sick as a dog in bed in my motel room all morning. It must have been food poisoning."

"You're going to be even sicker if I find out you had anything to do with this," Joe warned him as he followed Vanessa back to the car.

Joe and Vanessa followed the sound of sirens to the field where the *Beauty* had gone down. They arrived just behind a police car and an ambulance. The door of the police car opened, and Con Riley stepped out.

"Officer Riley," Joe called as he and Vanessa got out of the car. "Over here."

"Joe!" Riley said with surprise. "What do you know about this?"

"We saw the whole thing from the airfield coffee shop," Joe answered.

"I'll want to ask you some questions later," Riley said. "Right now, let's find out what we're dealing with."

Joe, Vanessa, and Riley followed the paramedics into the field. The *Beauty* was sitting in the dirt with its nose facing the road—dusty, but in one piece.

A tall young man with brown hair stood beside the plane. Joe's mouth fell open. "Frank!" he cried, running toward him. "What are you doing here?"

Frank left Cooper, who was still in the cockpit, to the paramedics and came forward to meet his brother. "Cooper took me up with him," he explained, looking a little dazed. "I landed the plane. It was awesome!"

"And Cooper?" Joe asked incredulously.

"He hit his nose and blacked out, but otherwise he's all right."

Joe stared at his brother for a moment, then cried, "You lunatic! I can't believe you pulled it off! We were in the coffee shop watching when the *Beauty* went down. I was sure she was going to be totaled."

"So was I!" Frank said, still looking stunned. "It was luck, pure and simple."

Joe looked back at the plane. The paramedics were helping a shaky Cooper out. Despite the blood and bruises on his face, he was smiling. He met Frank's eyes and gave a thumbs-up sign.

"It's been quite a day," Joe said, sitting in the Hardys' kitchen with his brother and sipping Aunt Gertrude's chicken soup.

After the crash, Joe and Frank had talked to Con Riley, filling him in on everything they knew. He took down all the information and radioed the station to be on the lookout for the *Killer Diller*. It had to land sometime, he said, and when it did the police had a few questions they wanted to ask the mystery pilot.

Riley had also gotten the fingerprint results back from the lab. There were no fingerprints on the crowbar, which indicated that the person who had broken into the Quonset hut probably knew enough to wear gloves or wipe the crowbar clean.

Frank took another sip of soup as the phone rang. He reached across the table to answer it. "Hello?"

"Hi, Frank," Vanessa said. "I just left the hospital. Uncle Brett's nose is broken, but otherwise he's fine."

"How are his spirits?" Frank asked.

"He's bossing around the nurses and telling everyone who will listen that he's going to kill the moron who hedge-hopped him."

Frank chuckled. "Sounds like everything's back to normal."

"Yes, except for one thing. The pit crew had the *Beauty* towed back to the airfield. It turns out the right wheel strut was bent during your descent."

"Oh, no!" Frank exclaimed. "I was afraid something like that might have happened."

"Uncle Brett can't afford to fix it," Vanessa continued. "He's going to take off and land on the crooked wheel and hope for the best."

"But that's dangerous!"

"I know. Mom tried to tell him that, but he won't listen. One more thing," she added. "I didn't think of this until just a couple of minutes ago. When I left Dixie today, she said she was heading over to the *Killer Diller* to talk to Cameron Diller. She might have seen who took his plane."

"Or maybe she was the one who hedge-hopped us," Frank suggested.

"I don't believe it!" Vanessa retorted. "After talking to Dixie today, I'm convinced she would never do anything to hurt Uncle Brett."

"I hope you're right, Vanessa," Frank said. "But until we find out who's behind this, everyone's a suspect."

*   *   *

The air was crisp and cool and the sky was clear blue when Frank and Joe arrived at the airfield the next morning. The section three crowd, including Vanessa and her mother, were out in force, and there was a feeling of growing excitement in the air. Overhead, Dixie was flying her pink biplane in lazy corkscrews.

"Today is the day, folks!" the announcer exclaimed over the loudspeaker as the Hardys walked to the ramp. "For the first time since this event began, we're going to see the Unlimited planes race against each other. Heat number one, featuring Brett Cooper's amazing new *Beauty,* starts in less than forty-five minutes."

"Hey, there's Con Riley," Joe said, hurrying to join him at the edge of the grandstands. "Officer Riley, I didn't know you were an aviation fan."

"I'm not," Riley said. "I'm here to see what I can find out about yesterday's incident."

"Has Diller's plane been recovered yet?" Frank asked.

"We found the *Killer Diller* early this morning. It landed in a field about twenty miles south of here."

"Did you find out who was flying it?" Joe asked.

Riley shook his head. "We dusted the cockpit for fingerprints, but we couldn't come up with any. All we found was a cigarette butt on the seat—Diller's brand—and a few flakes of loose tobacco on the floor.''

"Loose tobacco," Frank said. "Same as we found on Cooper's computer.''

"But that was probably from Cooper's cigarette,'' Joe reminded him. "And it's obvious Cooper wasn't flying the *Killer Diller*.''

"True. So I suppose the tobacco was from Diller's cigarette.''

"That's what we figured,'' Riley said. "Anyway, we questioned Diller, but he swears he has no idea who was flying his plane yesterday. And considering what an inconvenience it's been for him to get it out of that field and back here in time for his heat, I believe him.''

Frank and Joe left Riley and made their way to the *Beauty*. Frank found the pilot in the motor home, sitting at the kitchen table. Two strips of surgical tape held his broken nose in place.

"Good morning, Mr. Cooper,'' Frank began. "How are you feeling?''

"My nose hurts like all get out,'' Cooper growled.

"Do you have any idea who might have hedge-hopped us yesterday?'' Frank asked.

"It was Diller,'' Cooper said firmly.

"But he—''

"He might not have been flying the plane, but he set the whole thing up. Just wait until we get up in the air. I've got plans for Cameron Diller.''

"Vanessa told me about the wheel strut,''

Frank said. "Are you sure you ought to race today?"

"Of course I'm sure," Cooper snapped. "I've got to show the world what the *Beauty* can do."

"But your qualifying laps already proved the *Beauty* can fly faster than any of the other Unlimiteds," Joe said. "Isn't that enough?"

"That qualifying lap got everyone's attention," Cooper said. "Now I've got to prove it was no fluke."

"But landing with a bent wheel strut is dangerous!" Joe insisted.

"Unlimited air racing is dangerous," Cooper shot back. "Now go on. I've got a race to run."

Frank watched anxiously as the *Beauty* took off. The damaged wheel strut made the plane vibrate furiously, but she lifted off without mishap.

"Flying in heat number one with *Brett's Beauty* will be Lyle Freemont in *Wild Child*, Cameron Diller in *Killer Diller*, and Bob Trancas in his blue and white F4U-4 Corsair, *Miss Minnie*," the announcer told the crowd.

Down in the pit, Frank and Joe waited with Stan and Jesse for the race to begin. Stan carried a walkie-talkie that he used to communicate with Cooper.

"Pit to *Beauty*," Stan said into the radio. "All systems go? Over."

"A-okay," Frank heard Cooper reply.

All the pilots, their crews, and the control tower were tuned to the same frequency, Stan explained. According to racing rules, pilots were required to let their competitors know when they were about to pass another plane. They were also required to call Mayday in case of an emergency.

Frank watched the *Beauty* circle above the course while the other three planes took off. They were followed by the race starter, Jack Larsen, in an AT-6 World War II trainer plane.

All four Unlimiteds lined up behind the AT-6. Larsen's voice came over the radio. "*Wild Child*, you're too low, ease it up. *Beauty,* slow it down. *Miss Minnie*, tighten it up on the end."

The planes lumbered into line. "Okay, gentlemen, we're over the ridge at two hundred feet. Line up abreast. Final power increase coming on . . . now!"

Frank felt his heart drum with excitement as the Unlimiteds roared toward the first pylon. The AT-6 pulled up sharply, and Larsen uttered the ritual words, "Gentlemen, you have a race!"

The *Beauty* was in the lead as she passed the first pylon. Frank watched as Cooper screeched around it and headed for pylon two.

"*Brett's Beauty* takes the lead," the announcer said over the loudspeakers. "*Killer Diller* is second, then *Miss Minnie*, followed by *Wild Child*."

The racers shot around the course and headed for the second lap.

"*Wild Child* to *Miss Minnie*," Freemont's voice buzzed over the radio. "Passing on left."

Wild Child zoomed past *Miss Minnie* and headed toward the *Killer Diller*. In front of them all, *Brett's Beauty* banked ninety degrees and roared around the pylon to start lap three.

"Look at 'em go, folks!" the announcer cried. "And listen to this: we clocked the *Beauty* at five hundred twelve miles per hour! Ooh-wee, that baby is moving!"

Five laps later, the *Beauty* was still in front. Frank watched in awe as Cooper piloted his plane gracefully around the course. At the base of the first pylon, a referee waved a white flag, indicating the start of the final lap.

Diller turned on the juice and began to close the gap between his plane and the *Beauty*. Seconds later, the *Killer* was on Cooper's tail.

Stan and Jesse let out a frustrated groan. "Come on, Coop!" Jesse shouted to the sky. "Hold it, hold it!"

But the *Killer Diller* was still accelerating. Frank waited to hear Diller announce that he was about to pass. But to his surprise, Diller simply shot above the *Beauty* and overtook her.

"That's a penalty!" Jesse cried. "That's—"

But before he could say another word, Cooper's voice came over the radio. "What the—? *Beauty* to pit, *Beauty* to pit. I can't—"

Suddenly, Cooper's voice cut out. Frank gasped as an instant later the *Beauty* pulled up hard—right into the *Killer Diller*'s horizontal stabilizer. The *Beauty*'s right propeller caught the edge of the stabilizer's left elevator flap, ripping it off.

Frank stared in horror as the *Killer Diller* pitched sideways and corkscrewed toward the earth.

"Oh, no!" the announcer shouted. "He's going down! He's going down!"

Seconds later, the *Killer Diller* crashed nose first into the ground and burst into flames.

Chapter

10

JOE STARED, weak-kneed, as wild red and orange flames engulfed the *Killer Diller*. Black smoke filled the air.

The fire fighters waiting at the edge of the pit had already sprung into action. They drove their truck at top speed across the fields toward the burning plane. An ambulance barreled behind them.

Up in the sky, *Brett's Beauty* and the other racers roared past the last pylon to complete the final lap. Cooper won by three plane lengths, but Joe barely noticed. He was too concerned about the *Killer Diller* to care about anything else.

"What happened?" Frank asked in bewilderment. "I don't get it."

The announcer seemed to be wondering the

same thing. "It appears Cameron Diller passed without warning Brett Cooper," he told the crowd. "But why Cooper pulled up into him, I can't figure."

The fire fighters sprayed the downed plane with gallons of water. At the same time, the paramedics pushed their way into the wreck, searching for Diller's body.

Joe held his breath, waiting to see if Diller was still alive. His question was soon answered.

"The paramedics have just radioed us with some tragic news," the announcer said. "Cameron Diller is dead."

The crowd let out a collective gasp. Some of Diller's female fans burst into tears. Joe hung his head. "I may not have liked him," he said, "but I never would have wished this on him." Frank nodded grimly.

Moments later, *Brett's Beauty* landed unsteadily but safely on her damaged wheel strut. Cooper taxied into the pit, and Stan, Jesse, Frank, and Joe rushed forward to meet him.

Cooper lifted the canopy. A smoky sulfur smell drifted out of the cockpit. Cooper threw off his helmet. His face was pale, and there were tears in his eyes. "It was an accident," he said hopelessly. "I didn't mean to do it."

"What happened?" Frank asked.

"I don't know," Cooper said. "It happened so fast. All I know is that I was flying along, and all of a sudden I heard a loud popping noise.

Smoke shot out of the control panel, right into my eyes. I jumped back and covered my eyes, and the next thing I knew I was colliding with Diller's tail. I grabbed the joystick, pulled back on course, and crossed the finish line.''

"You won, Brett," Stan said quietly. "You dusted them."

"Did I?" Brett answered in a shaky voice. He smiled weakly. "Yeah, I guess I did."

Before anyone could say anything else, a pylon judge in a black and white striped shirt ran up and said, "Mr. Cooper, please come with us. The race committee would like to ask you a few questions."

Cooper climbed out of his plane and trudged off toward the control tower. Seconds later, a group of reporters surrounded Stan and Jesse, eager to get their take on the situation.

Frank and Joe took the opportunity to look over the *Beauty*'s control panel. The smoky sulfur smell was almost gone.

"It smells like caps from a cap gun," Joe said.

"Look at this," Frank remarked, pointing to a black, burned area around the edge of the oil temperature gauge.

"So you think Cooper was telling the truth?"

Frank frowned. "Until now, I believed everything he told us. Now I'm beginning to wonder. I mean, how many accidents can one pilot have?"

"You don't think it was sabotage?" Joe asked.

"Maybe. But who could have gotten near the *Beauty* long enough to plant a smoke bomb behind the oil temperature gauge—except Cooper himself?"

"Are you saying Cooper sabotaged his own plane?"

"Maybe. He'd need an alibi if he was planning to KO Diller, right?"

Joe looked dubious. "You think Cooper hated Diller enough to knock him out of the sky?"

"I'm not sure. But who had the opportunity to sabotage the *Beauty?* Cooper was in or near his plane all day yesterday. Plus, he's been sleeping in the motor home."

"Not last night," Joe pointed out. "He was in the hospital, remember?"

"Oh, that's right," Frank said, snapping his fingers. "So you're saying you think he's innocent?"

Joe shrugged. "Cooper wanted revenge for that hedge-hopping incident. That gives him a motive."

"Plus, I always get the feeling he's hiding something," Frank added. "Like when you asked him about that insurance policy. It didn't sound right."

Joe rubbed his face with his hands. "I don't know what to think," he said wearily.

The Hardys found the Benders in section three, arguing with their friends about the accident. Most of the crowd seemed to feel the crash was Cooper's fault.

"But Diller didn't announce he was passing," Mrs. Bender argued. "Brett had no idea the *Killer Diller* was above him."

Frank and Joe sat down beside Vanessa. Joe slipped his arm around her shoulders.

"Isn't it awful?" she said. She looked out over the race course.

Joe pulled Vanessa close to him. "Cooper says he pulled up accidentally. He didn't know Diller was there."

Just then, the announcer's voice broke in. "Ladies and gentlemen, the race committee has ruled that Brett Cooper was not to blame. Cameron Diller neglected to signal a pass. His death was a regrettable and tragic accident."

He paused, letting his words sink in. There were scattered boos and angry hisses, but gradually the crowd fell silent.

"Here are the final race results," the announcer continued somberly. *"Brett's Beauty* came in first at an average speed of five hundred two miles per hour. That's a record, folks. *Wild Child* was in second place, and *Miss Minnie* brought up the rear."

The announcer droned on. "Let's go home," Mrs. Bender said. "I don't want to see any more."

"You go ahead," Vanessa said. "I'm going to stick around with Joe and Frank."

Mrs. Bender gave Vanessa a hug and left for the parking lot.

"Let's see what's going on with the *Beauty*," Joe suggested. The three of them headed for the ramp.

"Frank! Joe!" a familiar voice suddenly called. "Hey, wait up!"

Frank, Joe, and Vanessa spun around to find themselves face to face with Ray Kolinsky. "Ray!" Frank exclaimed. He looked closely at Ray's small, dark eyes. Could he have been the one flying *Killer Diller,* or the one who planted the smoke bomb in the *Beauty?*

"You asked me to try to remember if anything unusual happened around the time Brett quit racing," Ray said.

Joe nodded. "Go on."

"Well, I thought and thought, and finally something came to me. One morning Brett and I were in his barn in Mansfield, working on the *Beauty*. We heard a truck pull up outside, and Brett went out to see who it was. He came back a few minutes later carrying a Federal Express letter. He had this look on his face like he'd just gotten the worst news of his life."

"Did he say what it was?" Joe asked.

Ray shook his head. "I asked, but he said it was nothing. I had to wonder though. He looked stunned, just wasted. But he pulled himself together and we got back to work." Ray paused.

"About a week later, Brett announced he was quitting racing."

"Did you ever ask him about that letter again?" Frank asked.

"No. Like I told you, Brett's a real private guy. If he doesn't want to talk about something, wild horses can't drag it out of him."

"Thanks, Ray," Frank said. "You've been a big help."

Ray sighed. "Man, these last couple of days have been brutal—watching Brett race and knowing I can't be a part of it. It's killing me."

Looking into Ray's sad, empty eyes, Frank believed him. "We'll let you know if we learn anything important," he said.

"All right!" Joe exclaimed as Ray faded into the crowd. "At last we're onto something."

"That's my Joe," Vanessa remarked. "Just give him an interesting clue and he's happy."

"Come on," Frank said, grabbing their arms and leading them across the ramp. "Let's find out what Dixie knows about this mysterious letter."

"A Federal Express letter?" Dixie asked, bewildered. "No, I can't remember anything like that."

Joe's face fell. "Are you sure?"

Dixie was sitting in her biplane, getting ready to entertain the crowd before the start of the second heat.

"Brett was always getting deliveries—engine parts form Zable Aviation, letters from other airplane designers—all kinds of things," she said.

"But do you remember him acting any differently about a week before he decided to quit racing?" Vanessa asked.

"Nothing specific," she replied as Lyle handed her the goggles. "Although now that you mention it, it was about that time he started carrying that silly briefcase."

"What briefcase?" Frank asked.

"It was a handmade deerskin one," Dixie said. "He said he bought it to hold all his important papers, but I could never understand what the big deal was. 'Why not use a file cabinet like other people?' I asked him." She shook her head. "He never let it out of his sight. He wouldn't even let *me* touch it."

"I remember seeing that briefcase in Cooper's motor home," Frank said.

"One more question," Joe said. "Do you think the crash today was an accident?"

Dixie thought a moment. "A few years ago, I would have said definitely. Brett is a tough competitor, but he always played by the rules. Now, I don't know. Brett's changed. He cares more about the *Beauty* than anything in this world—including me."

Dixie pulled the throttle and slowly taxied toward the runway. "Are you coming up with me later?" she called to Vanessa.

"I wouldn't miss it for the world!" Vanessa shouted back.

As Dixie took off, Frank, Joe, and Vanessa turned to each other. They were all thinking the same thing.

"Uncle Brett isn't going to let you near that briefcase," Vanessa said.

"Then we'll have to sneak into the motor home and look for it ourselves," Joe replied.

"But those are Uncle Brett's private papers," Vanessa said anxiously. "You can't go through them behind his back."

'Vanessa, a man died today," Frank said seriously. "We have to solve this case before someone else gets hurt. Besides, if Cooper is innocent, he has nothing to hide. And if he isn't—well, we have to find out."

Vanessa thought it over. "Come on," she said firmly. "Let's do what we have to do."

Frank led the way to the *Beauty*'s pit. Stan was on the wing, looking over the airplane's engine, while Jesse sat in the cockpit, repairing the oil temperature gauge. Fans with pit passes stood behind the barriers, gawking. At least a dozen reporters were there, too, hoping for a quote or a new angle on the crash.

Off to the side, Frank noticed Officer Riley and Police Chief Collig talking to Brett Cooper.

"Looks as if the police decided to do their own investigation of the crash," Joe said.

"You and Vanessa go over and keep them talking," Frank said. "I'm going to find that briefcase."

Frank looked around to make sure no one was paying attention to him. Then he slipped into the motor home and searched for the deerskin briefcase. He found it in a closet, behind Cooper's jackets and jeans.

There was a small lock on the clasp, but Frank quickly picked it with a paper clip he found on the table. Inside, Frank found Cooper's life-insurance policy, along with his divorce papers, some receipts, and blueprints of the *Beauty*.

The center section of the briefcase was zipped shut. Frank unzipped it and pulled out five or six loose white papers with typewritten messages on them. He was careful not to get his fingerprints on them. As he read them, his mouth fell open.

"QUIT RACING IMMEDIATELY," the first one said, "OR YOUR WIFE WILL HAVE AN ACCIDENT. KEEP QUIET ABOUT THIS."

Frank picked up the second one. "THIS IS SERIOUS," it read. "IF YOU RACE AGAIN, YOUR WIFE WILL DIE."

"I'M STILL WATCHING," the third one read. "NO RACING, NO TALKING TO THE COPS OR YOU CAN KISS DIXIE GOODBYE."

Chapter

11

FRANK SKIMMED the rest of the blackmail letters. Each one warned that Dixie would be killed if Cooper continued racing. Quickly, Frank slipped the first letter into his pocket. Then he put the others back, returned the briefcase to the closet, and hurried outside.

Joe and Vanessa were at the edge of the pit, talking with Cooper, Chief Collig, and Officer Riley. Frank walked over to join them.

"Ah, Frank, there you are," Chief Collig said sternly. "Mr. Cooper was just telling me that you and your brother have been investigating some sabotage attempts on his airplane."

"Well, yes—" Frank began.

"I appreciate your enthusiasm, boys," Collig

continued, "but I think this is a matter best left to the police."

Frank glanced at his brother. He was dying to tell Joe about the blackmail letters. But it looked as if Chief Collig was revving up for a full-blown lecture. Fortunately, at that moment Jesse called, "Hey, Brett, check this out!"

Everyone hurried over to the *Beauty*. "What is it?" Cooper asked.

"I took apart the oil temperature gauge," Jesse answered. "It looks as if there was some kind of smoke bomb rigged up behind it. See," he said, pointing at a slender piece of charred wire. "When the oil temperature gauge registered high enough, the smoke bomb went off."

"I knew it," Cooper fumed. "It was a setup."

"But whoever did it couldn't have predicted the bomb would go off just as Diller passed you," Riley pointed out. "That was just an unfortunate coincidence."

"And a deadly one," Collig added gravely.

While Collig and Riley continued talking to Cooper and Jesse, Frank pulled Joe and Vanessa aside.

"Did you find the briefcase?" Joe asked.

"Did I!" Frank pulled the letter out of his shirt. "Look at this!"

"Poor Uncle Brett," Vanessa said with a worried frown after she read the note.

"There's one thing I don't get," Joe said.

"Why do you suppose Cooper decided to start racing again?"

"Maybe the blackmail letters stopped," Frank suggested. "Or maybe he's so obsessed with the *Beauty,* he decided to risk it."

"No way!" Vanessa protested. "No matter how obsessed Uncle Brett is, he'd never do anything to put Dixie's life in danger."

Out of the corner of his eye, Frank noticed Chief Collig and Officer Riley leaving. "Officer Riley, can I talk to you a second?" he called.

Riley walked over. "What's up, guys?"

"Look at this," Frank said.

Riley glanced at the letter. "Holy cow!" he exclaimed. "Where did you find this?"

"In Cooper's briefcase," Frank admitted. "Can you take it to the police lab and have it analyzed?"

"Sure. I'll let you know what I find out. But don't expect this letter back. Blackmail is a federal offense, you know. I'll have to send it to the FBI."

"With any luck, we'll have this case wrapped up before then," Frank said, sounding more confident than he felt.

"What now?" Vanessa asked after Riley had left.

"It's time to talk to Cooper," Joe said. "Mr. Cooper," he called, "can we have a word with you?"

Cooper was leaning over the *Beauty*'s engine

103

with Stan and Jesse. "Can't you see I'm busy?" he growled.

"Mr. Cooper, we don't have time to play games," Frank said firmly. "Please come into the motor home. *Now.*"

Cooper threw down a socket wrench. "This had better be good."

Cooper strode into the motor home and opened the refrigerator. It was empty. He cursed and slammed the door. Then he took out a cigarette, the last in the pack, and lit it.

"Mr. Cooper," Frank began, "we know about the blackmail letters."

"What?" Cooper said. "What are you talking about?"

"The letters in your briefcase," Frank continued. "I read them."

"You went through my personal papers!" Cooper stormed. He clenched his fist and took a step toward Frank.

Vanessa moved forward and grabbed his arm. "Uncle Brett, stop! I know it was wrong, but what were we supposed to do? You want us to find out who's sabotaging your plane, but you're withholding important information from us."

Cooper scowled, then slowly lowered his arm. "All right, all right." He sat down and inhaled on his cigarette. "I got the first letter about four years ago, and after that a new one came every six months like clockwork. What could I do? I

104

loved Dixie, and I would have done anything to protect her. So I quit racing."

"Did you tell anyone about the letters?" Joe asked.

"No one. I didn't want to do anything that might put Dixie in danger."

"If you're so concerned about Dixie, why are you racing again?" Joe asked.

"After Dixie divorced me, I hit rock bottom. I loved her, you know." He sighed. "I guess I still do. But then I thought, what if everyone thought I hated her? The blackmailer might give up, because I don't have any other family. The only person left to threaten is me, and that's a risk I'm willing to take to prove to the world what the *Beauty* can do."

"Well, that would explain why someone programmed your plane to shut down for ten seconds," Joe said. "And the hedge-hopping incident, too."

"Not to mention what happened today," Vanessa added. "Someone's determined to make you stop racing."

"Hold on," Frank broke in. "Have you received any blackmail letters threatening that harm would come to you if you competed in the Bayport race?"

"No," Cooper admitted. "The last letter I got was months ago, and it referred to Dixie."

"What I don't get is why anyone would want

to stop you from racing in the first place," Vanessa said.

Cooper shrugged. "If I can't race, I can't win. And that leaves first place—and the prize money—to some other pilot." He reached into his breast pocket for a cigarette and came up with an empty package. "Darn it all!" he barked, tossing the crumpled pack aside. "I'm so broke, I can't even afford cigarettes."

"Good," Vanessa said with satisfaction. "It's time for you to quit."

Frank and Joe were relaxing in front of the television until five o'clock, when they planned to help Cooper and the crew work on the *Beauty*. The Hardys had stayed at the airfield the rest of the morning. While they'd watched the second and third heats, Vanessa had received her second flying lesson from Dixie. Then Vanessa went home with her mother.

Frank reached for a potato chip as the phone rang. "Every time we try to catch some hang time, the phone rings," he said, picking up the portable. "Hello?"

"Frank? This is Con Riley. I asked the lab to do a rush job on that blackmail letter. All the fingerprints were identical, so you can figure they belong to Brett Cooper."

"Anything else?" Frank asked eagerly.

"Yes. The boys in the lab say the letters were written on a 1952 Brentwood typewriter. Brent-

wood was a small company with a slightly unusual typeface. They're out of business now.
Anyway, if you look closely, you'll notice the
letter Q is a little crooked, which means the Q
key on this particular typewriter must be slightly
bent."

Frank's spirits leaped. "Thanks," he said.
"Now all we have to do is find the typewriter."

"You might as well look for a needle in a hay-
stack," Riley said. "That typewriter could be
anywhere in the country."

"Thanks for your encouragement," Frank
said.

"Be realistic, Frank," Riley said. "Leave this
one to the FBI."

"The Feds are going to need all the help they
can get, so we're not quitting," Frank replied.

When Frank and Joe arrived at the pit that
evening, they found Cooper in the motor home,
talking with George Zable. Both men were smoking fat cigars.

"George, you know Frank Hardy," Cooper
said. "And this is his brother, Joe. Joe, this is
George Zable."

"How do you do, sir," Joe said, shaking his
hand.

"I just took your boss out for a prime rib dinner," Zable said. "I think it's the first decent
meal he's had in weeks."

"I'm not going to be poor much longer," Cooper said with dignity. "After the Gold race, the offers will start pouring in."

"I'm kind of surprised they haven't already," Frank remarked. "The *Beauty* has flown twice so far, and both times she's broken a speed record. Isn't that enough to convince the aviation companies you've created something special?"

It was Zable, not Cooper, who answered. "The *Beauty*'s speed is impressive," he said, puffing on his cigar. "But if you're hoping to cross over to the commercial market, reliability is even more important. In the time trials, the *Beauty* had computer problems. In the heat race, the oil temperature gauge blew."

"But both of those incidents were sabotage!" Cooper protested. "The *Beauty* has a superb reliability record."

"You don't have to convince me," Zable said. "I'm just telling you what I've been hearing around the airfield. People are saying the *Beauty*'s engine is too temperamental to use for anything except air racing, and maybe not even that."

Cooper looked as if someone had slapped him in the face. "It's not true," he said, but without his usual conviction. "The *Beauty* is going to revolutionize small-aircraft aviation."

Zable patted him on the shoulder. "Hey, I'm on your side, remember? I think the sponsorship deal I offered you proves that." He stood up and walked out the door, still puffing on his cigar.

Frank and Joe looked at Cooper. The proud, confident pilot with the growling voice and quick temper had disappeared. In his place was a husky man with rounded shoulders and tired eyes.

"Mr. Cooper," Frank asked, "are you thinking of accepting Mr. Zable's sponsorship offer?"

"I don't know," Cooper answered. "If I want to stay out of bankruptcy court, I might have to." He sighed. "Take a look at this."

Cooper opened his deerskin briefcase and handed Frank and Joe a piece of paper. It was a letter from a Mansfield, Pennsylvania, collection agency warning Cooper that unless he paid his creditors in ten days, he would be taken to court and all his assets would be seized.

"You mean they could take your farm away from you?" Joe asked.

Cooper laughed bitterly. "I sold my farm before I came here to pay off a stack of other debts." He smiled wanly. "I only have one asset left. The *Beauty*."

"It looks like sponsorship is the only reasonable choice left," Frank said.

Cooper nodded. "At least I know I can trust Zable. He's stuck by me when my closest friends and family haven't."

Frank knew Cooper was referring to Ray and Dixie. But had they truly betrayed him? Or had his temperamental nature driven them away?

Cooper put out his cigar and got to his feet.

"Stan and Jesse should be here by now. Let's get to work."

Frank and Joe followed him outside. To their surprise, they saw a stranger sitting in the *Beauty*'s cockpit. He was wearing gray coveralls and an orange motorcycle helmet with the visor flipped up.

"It's him!" Frank hissed. "The same guy we caught in the Quonset hut."

"Hey!" Cooper shouted. "Get away from there!"

The man flipped down his visor, then leaped out of the cockpit and took off across the ramp.

"I'm on it," Joe said to his brother. "You check out the *Beauty*." He disappeared after the helmeted intruder.

Frank and Cooper ran to the plane and looked inside the cockpit. Everything was as Stan and Jesse had left it. Then Frank noticed a few flakes of tobacco scattered across the seat. He picked up a piece and rolled it between his fingers. "This is tobacco from your cigarettes, right?" he asked.

Cooper looked closely. "I don't think so. It looks like chewing tobacco to me."

Chewing tobacco. The words bounced around Frank's brain. Who do I know who chews tobacco? he asked himself.

Then suddenly, something clicked. "Lyle Freemont!" he exclaimed.

Chapter

12

THE HELMETED MAN who had been in the *Beauty* ran across the ramp. He was a tall, lanky man with a smooth, even stride. Joe ran after him, his muscular legs pumping and his heart pounding in his chest.

It was after five o'clock, and the pits were mostly deserted. A few crew workers glanced up as the helmeted man ran by with Joe in hot pursuit.

The man dodged behind a purple Mustang. Joe followed, but the man seemed to have disappeared.

Joe stopped, panting hard, and looked around. A second later, he saw the man dart out of the shadows almost fifty yards away.

Joe ran after him, and once again the gap between them began to close. But the mysterious man clearly knew his way around the airfield. Again, Joe lost sight of him, and stopped.

Then suddenly, Joe caught a glimpse of him at the edge of the ramp. The man was heading for the parking lot.

Joe took off running. As he entered the lot, he saw an orange and blue dirt bike parked at the end of one of the rows. Joe sped up, catching up with the man just yards from the bike. The two of them hit the ground, breathing hard. As Joe reached for the tinted visor that hid the stranger's face, the man sat up abruptly, whacking Joe in the forehead with his helmet.

Joe reeled backward, stunned. Instantly, the man was on his feet. He jumped on his cycle and started the engine. Joe struggled to his feet as the stranger kicked the bike into gear.

Desperately, Joe lunged forward and leaped onto the man's back. At the same moment, the stranger revved the accelerator. The dirt bike shot forward, swerving wildly. Joe tried to hold on, but his legs were hanging off the back of the bike. One of his hightops dragged across the asphalt.

Suddenly, the man raised his left arm and swung his elbow into Joe's ribs.

Joe gasped as searing pain shot through his chest. Just then, the bike hit a bump and Joe's hands slipped. He hit the asphalt and rolled three times before he came to a stop. Slowly, painfully, he lifted his head and watched the dirt bike turn onto the main road and disappear.

While Stan and Jesse repaired the oil temperature gauge, Frank and Cooper went into the motor home to talk.

"Do you think Freemont really hates you enough to sabotage the *Beauty?*" Frank asked.

"I wouldn't put it past him," Cooper replied. "He never forgave me for winning that race. And he thinks I'm the one who got him disqualified."

"But that was four years ago," Frank pointed out.

"He's not one to forgive and forget. Besides, who knows what Dixie has been telling him about me? Maybe Freemont thinks he's avenging her honor or some fool thing."

Frank thought it over. "But could Freemont have been responsible for those sabotage attempts back in Pennsylvania?"

"Who knows?" Cooper said impatiently. "After I quit racing, I never saw him anymore. If he was in Mansfield, I didn't know it."

"One more question," Frank said. "The police said the blackmail letters were written on an antique 1952 Brentwood typewriter. Does that sound like something Freemont would own?"

Cooper shook his head. "Freemont likes everything sleek and new, like that souped-up Corvette he drives. The only antique he owns is his plane.''

Suddenly, the door opened, and Joe limped in. His shirt was torn, and there was a large scrape on his left hand.

"What happened?" Frank asked in alarm.

"He got away," Joe said glumly. He touched his tender ribs and winced. "I sure wish I knew who that dude was."

"We've got a pretty good idea," Frank answered. He reached into his shirt pocket and pulled out a few shreds of tobacco. "We found this on the seat of the *Beauty*. It's chewing tobacco . . . Lyle Freemont chews tobacco."

"Lyle Freemont!" Joe set his jaw. "Freemont," he said darkly, "I'm coming to get you."

The next morning, Frank and Joe picked up Vanessa and headed to the airfield.

"So what's our next step?" Vanessa asked.

"Find Lyle Freemont and follow him," Frank said.

"And hope he does something incriminating, like tamper with the *Beauty*," Joe added eagerly.

Their first stop was the *Wild Child*'s pit. There was no sign of Freemont there, so they headed for the coffee shop. Freemont was at the counter, drinking coffee and trading gossip with the other pilots. He glanced up as they walked in.

"Good morning, Mr. Freemont," Frank said pleasantly.

"Howdy, son," Freemont replied, touching the brim of his cowboy hat.

"Thanks for the bruises," Joe whispered under his breath as they sat down at a nearby booth. "Hope I can return the favor someday."

Vanessa nudged Joe into silence. They ordered coffee and eavesdropped on the pilot's conversation.

"Go on, Lyle," one of the pilots said. "Who told you the *Beauty* wasn't reliable?"

"Nobody had to tell me," Freemont replied. "Just look at her. She's had problems since day one." He laughed. "The future of small aircraft aviation! Give me a break!"

"But Cooper says his plane was sabotaged," said a man in a *Miss Minnie* cap.

Lyle laughed shortly. "He'll say anything to sell his design. He's broke, remember?"

Vanessa and the Hardys exchanged a meaningful look. Zable had said there was talk around the airfield that the *Beauty* was unreliable. Now they knew where it was coming from.

"Every new plane has problems," another pilot remarked. "It takes a while to get the bugs out."

"Granted, but the *Beauty*'s had problems since the beginning," Freemont insisted. "George Zable told me Cooper ordered three turbochargers from his company in six months. The darned engine destroyed them."

Frank shot a puzzled glance at Joe. Was Zable bad-mouthing Cooper, too?

When Freemont left, Frank, Joe, and Vanessa followed him back to the *Wild Child* pit. A few minutes later, Freemont headed across the ramp to the hangars with Frank, Joe, and Vanessa following at a safe distance. When Freemont went into hangar three, they peered in to see what was going on.

Zable was standing beside a Cessna 172 airplane. He and Freemont talked for a minute. The Hardys and Vanessa could only make out a few words—"totally fooled," "good job," and "Cooper belongs to me." Then Zable opened a briefcase and took out a thick wad of cash.

"Excuse me, kids," a voice said. "Are you looking for someone?"

Frank, Joe, and Vanessa spun around to find a security guard gazing at them suspiciously. "Uh, no, sir," Frank said. "We're just—"

"This hangar is off limits," he said. "Even for the pit crews. It's the private property of Zable Aviation."

The security guard watched as Frank, Joe, and Vanessa walked away. "Now we'll never know what that money was for," Frank said.

"Get real," Joe shot back. "Zable was paying Freemont off."

"You mean you think Mr. Zable hired Freemont to sabotage the *Beauty?*" Vanessa asked.

Frank thought it over. "Maybe. But the question is, why?"

Joe frowned. "What do you say we head over to Zable Aviation headquarters and see if they know anything about a 1952 Brentwood typewriter with a busted Q?"

Zable Aviation was located just north of Bayport. Frank parked the van in the visitors' lot and walked into the main office with Joe and Vanessa. He found himself in a spacious room with deep burgundy carpeting and large windows. The walls were decorated with photographs of Zable aircraft.

A white-haired receptionist with glasses and pinched lips sat behind an elegant teak desk, bearing a sign that said his name was Mr. Wardle. Behind him, three secretaries answered telephones and typed at computer terminals. To the left Frank noticed a corridor leading to more offices.

"Let me handle this," Vanessa whispered. She walked up to the receptionist. "Good morning. I'm wondering if you can help me."

Mr. Wardle peered over his glasses. "Yes?"

"Last week a friend of my family received a letter from Zable Aviation typed on an old-fashioned typewriter. My mother and I own an antique shop, and we're always looking for interesting items. Could you tell me who owns that typewriter? We might want to make an offer."

117

Mr. Wardle frowned. "An antique typewriter? Impossible. Our offices are state of the art—completely computerized."

Frank could feel the moment slipping away. "Uh, is Mr. Zable in?" he asked.

"Mr. Zable is at the airfield. Now, if you'll excuse me, I have work to do."

Mr. Wardle turned back to his work, and the Hardys and Vanessa reluctantly headed for the door.

"We can forget about questioning the employees," Frank said glumly. "Security here is tighter than in most prisons."

At that moment, one of the secretaries who had been working behind Mr. Wardle walked out the office door. She was in her twenties, plump, with curly red hair. "Excuse me," she said, hurrying up to Joe. "Are you famous? I could swear I've seen you on TV."

Joe laughed. "I don't think so."

"Oh," she said with disappointment. "Well, you *should* be. You're cute!"

Joe grinned, half embarrassed, half pleased. "Uh, thanks."

"Listen, I overheard what you were saying to Mr. Wardle. I've never seen any old typewriters here, but Mr. Zable has a private office in New York City, and I've heard it's full of expensive antiques."

"Really?" Joe said. "Do you know the address?"

"Sure. We send mail there all the time. It's Four-forty West Forty-fifth Street."

"Thanks!" Joe said. "You've been a big help."

The secretary giggled and hurried back inside.

"You're cute!" Vanessa mimicked. She rolled her eyes. "Oh, puh-lease!" She poked Joe in the stomach.

"Hey, you guys," Frank interrupted, "we have to get moving. There's a mystery waiting to be solved."

It was usually a short commute from Bayport into Manhattan, but after stopping for gas and a late lunch, the Hardys and Vanessa were frustrated to find themselves caught in rush-hour traffic. Construction on the West Side Highway slowed them down even further.

It was after six o'clock when Frank found a parking space near their destination. The trio hurried into the lobby of the tall glass and steel skyscraper, only to discover that the elevators were shut down for the night.

"All closed up," a uniformed security guard told them. "Come back tomorrow morning at nine."

On the way out, they glanced at the directory and saw that George Zable's office was suite 662.

"Let's try the service entrance," Frank suggested.

They went around to the back of the building

and tried the service door. It was open! A heavy gray door led to the emergency stairs.

By the time they reached the sixth floor, they were all breathing hard. Frank opened the door and stepped into the corridor. No one was in sight, but the sound of a vacuum cleaner could be heard at the other end of the hall.

Frank motioned to Joe and Vanessa, and they tiptoed down the hall to suite 662. They stepped inside and flipped on the lights.

They were in the suite's reception area. The room was dominated by an antique oak desk and a pine table covered with papers and office supplies. Black and white photographs of antique airplanes lined the walls. On the desk was a modern computer terminal, but no typewriter.

While Vanessa paused to look at one of the photographs, Frank and Joe walked into the next room. They found an office that could have come out of the 1940s. On a small stand in the corner sat an old-fashioned typewriter. Frank and Joe hurried over. It was a Brentwood. Joe opened the cover and looked inside. The Q key was slightly bent.

The brothers grinned and wordlessly began searching the rest of the office.

"Hey, look!" Joe cried suddenly, waving a sheet of paper he had found in the bottom drawer of Zable's desk.

Frank took the paper from him. It was a signed contract between Zable Aviation and one of the country's biggest overnight mail services, Speedy Express. The contract promised to deliver two hundred Brett Cooper–designed airplanes to Speedy Express over the next two years.

"I don't get it," Frank mused. "How can Zable be so sure Cooper will let him use his design?"

"Good question," Joe said. "Cooper said he wasn't making any deals with airplane companies until after the Gold race. If that's true, this contract is illegal."

"Here's something else that's illegal," Frank said. "This is a signed contract dated September first. But today is only August sixteenth."

"Hey, Vanessa," Joe called, "look at—" Joe fell silent as a scuffling sound came from the next room. It was followed by Vanessa's muffled cry. Joe quickly put the contract back in the drawer. With hearts pounding, Joe and Frank ran into the reception area.

Vanessa was standing in the middle of the room. Lyle Freemont was directly behind her. One of his hands was pressed tightly over her mouth, while his other hand pinned her arm painfully behind her back.

"Don't move," he drawled, "or the girl gets hurt."

Chapter

13

FOR A MOMENT, Frank and Joe stood frozen in the suite. Then, Frank decided to take a chance that Freemont was unarmed. "I've got a gun!" he lied, thrusting his hand into the pocket of his jacket.

Startled, Freemont loosened his grip on Vanessa and took a small step backward. Joe took advantage of the moment, grabbing Vanessa's arm and pulling her toward him while simultaneously delivering a swift kick to Freemont's chest.

The pilot reeled backward. His cowboy hat flew off his head as he slammed against the wall. Instantly, Frank was on top of him, pinning his shoulders against the carpet.

"What are you doing here?" Joe demanded.

"And why did you sabotage Brett Cooper's plane?"

"Don't hurt me," Freemont whined. "It was a job, that's all. I needed the money."

"Who hired you?" Frank asked. "Zable?"

"Very good," said a voice from the hallway. "The boy detectives have done it again."

Everyone turned as George Zable walked into the room with a Browning high-powered automatic in his hand. He pointed the barrel at Frank's forehead. "Stand up, son."

Frank got up slowly and stepped away from Freemont. Zable motioned for Frank to move next to Joe. Frank exchanged a frustrated glance with Joe, who put his arm around Vanessa.

Freemont put his cowboy hat back on and scrambled to his feet.

"I received an interesting phone call from Mr. Wardle this afternoon," Zable said calmly, leveling his gun at three teenagers. "It seems he noticed one of my young secretaries talking to you. After questioning the young lady, Mr. Wardle learned the girl sent you here. Something about an antique typewriter?"

"A 1952 Brentwood with a bent Q key," Joe said. "The same one you used to type blackmail letters to Brett Cooper."

"Yes, I wrote those letters to stop Cooper from racing," Zable remarked, unperturbed. "I knew that he needed the winnings to finance his new plane. Without them, he'd be seriously strapped for money."

"Is that why Zable Aviation sent Brett Cooper defective speed-reduction gearboxes and turbochargers?" Frank asked. "To bankrupt him?"

"My, you *are* clever," Zable chuckled. "And you're right."

Freemont laughed. "Cooper's had to make so many repairs because of Diller and me over the last five years, he's in debt up to his eyeballs."

"So it was Diller who damaged the *Beauty* with a sledgehammer back at Cooper's farm," Frank said.

"Right," Freemont bragged. "And I did the rest. I changed the propeller bolt and set up Kolinsky to take the blame. Then I reprogrammed the computer and put the smoke bomb in the oil gauge. It was no problem finding the *Beauty*—I simply put a homing device on Cooper's jeep and he led me straight to the hut."

"We borrowed the *Killer Diller* for that little hedge-hopping incident," Zable said with satisfaction. "That was a nice touch, I think—making it seem as if Diller was the culprit."

"You'll never get away with this," Joe said between clenched teeth.

"I already have," Zable replied. "Cooper is a broken man—divorced, bankrupt, desperate."

"But what's the point?" Vanessa asked in frustration. "Why did you want to ruin Uncle Brett?"

"It's simple," Zable replied. "The first time Cooper showed me his design for the *Beauty*, I knew he was sitting on a potential gold mine. He wasn't interested in making me his partner, so I took action." He smiled and adjusted his string tie. "Now the only way Cooper can pay his debts is to sign over ninety-nine percent of the *Beauty* to me."

"Uncle Brett will never agree to that," Vanessa cried.

"What choice does he have?" Freemont drawled. "If he refuses, he'll have to hand the *Beauty* over to his creditors anyway."

"And one of those creditors is me," Zable said with satisfaction. "So you see, either way you slice it, Cooper loses. And I win."

"Why are you telling us all this?" Frank asked.

"Why not?" Zable said casually. "Once I dispose of the Brentwood typewriter, you'll have no evidence against me. Then all I have to do is return to Bayport and convince Cooper to sign a contract with me." He shrugged. "Considering the state he's in, that shouldn't be too hard."

"Unless we get there first and warn him," Vanessa said.

"No chance," Zable replied. "Lyle, cover us while I take the Hardys and their friend into my office and tie them up. We'll release them tomorrow after the Gold race."

"You got it, boss," Freemont said, taking

the gun. He motioned toward the connecting door.

"Zable," Frank said as they walked into the inner office, "don't fool yourself. Even without that typewriter, we've got plenty of evidence against you."

Joe knew his brother was bluffing, but what did they have to lose? "You too, Lyle," he said. "Dixie told us everything."

Freemont guffawed loudly. "Dixie? She doesn't have a clue."

"Don't you even love her?" Vanessa asked.

"Don't make me laugh. I needed to know about the *Beauty*'s computers. Dixie had helped Ray design the original programs. I took her out to dinner a few times and got her talking."

"Do sit down," Zable said, pointing to the three mahogany chairs in the middle of the room. Zable walked to the closet and, for a moment, turned his back to them.

Joe could sense his brother's thoughts. "You really know how to handle that dirt bike, Lyle," he said, hoping to distract the pilot. "Do you race it?"

"Since I was a kid," Freemont answered. With his free hand he reached down to open the leather pouch on his belt and take a pinch of tobacco.

That was the opening Frank was looking for. He lunged out of his chair, grabbed a heavy brass paperweight from the desk, and hurled it at Freemont's back. Freemont let out a shout of surprise.

Seeing his brother leap into action, Joe rushed to the closet and tackled Zable around the waist. Zable fell to the floor with Joe on top of him.

As Frank struggled with Freemont, the gun went off. The bullet flew past Joe's left shoulder, grazing him. With a groan, Joe rolled off Zable and hit the floor, clutching his wound. Frank backed away from the pilot, and Vanessa ran to Joe, kneeling down next to him.

"Sit down!" Freemont ordered.

"But Joe's been shot!" Vanessa cried.

Zable picked himself up off the floor and straightened his string tie. "That's not our concern," he said. "Sit."

Reluctantly, Frank and Vanessa did as they were told. Joe struggled to his feet and, still clutching his shoulder, sat beside them.

Zable returned to the closet and came back with three large spools of packing twine. With Freemont pointing the gun at the Hardys and Vanessa, Zable tied the three teenagers tightly to their chairs. Then he shoved wads of crumpled typing paper into their mouths and secured them with packing tape.

"Let's get out of here," Freemont said.

"Have a good evening, friends," Zable said, bowing graciously to his captives. "Sleep well."

* * *

The minutes ticked by. Frank sat in total darkness, feeling the uncomfortable pull of twine against his skin and the hard pressure of crumpled paper in his mouth. Beside him, he could hear Joe and Vanessa's fast, anxious breathing.

Frank tried to concentrate. There had to be a way to escape. He remembered he had heard the whine of a vacuum cleaner down the hall, but the custodians had probably left the building. Frank stared into the darkness, trying to remember everything he had seen in both the outer and inner offices. There had to be something he could use to cut the twine that bound him.

Suddenly, he remembered the pine table in the outer office. It was covered with papers and office equipment—an electric pencil sharpener, a fax machine, a hole puncher, and . . . a paper cutter. The paper cutter was about two feet by two feet with a long handle containing a sharp blade. If he could just get into the outer office!

Eagerly Frank began shimmying from side to side, swinging his hips slightly forward. His feet were tied together, and he was bound at the waist, with his hands tied behind his back. It was tough going, but slowly, his chair began to inch along. The mahogany chair was heavy, and the carpet created friction, but little by little, he could feel himself moving.

After what seemed like an eternity, Frank's chair bumped against the door. He edged forward and pressed his upper arm against the door-knob, rotating his shoulder to turn it.

No luck. He tried again and again, grunting in frustration.

Finally, on his fifth try, he turned the handle enough to open the door. With growing excitement, he inched toward the pine table. His muscles strained against the twine, and sweat poured off his face.

The dim strip of light that shone under the outer door allowed Frank to see the paper cutter. The blade was slightly raised. Frank rotated his chair so that his back was facing the cutter. By raising himself and stooping over, he was able to reach his hands out and under the blade. Then he began to rock back and forth, rubbing the twine against the blade.

It wasn't long before the prickly twine began to shred. Eagerly, Frank strained against his bonds until the twine snapped. In an instant, his hands were free!

Frank pulled the tape off his mouth and spit out the wad of paper. "Joe, Vanessa, hang tight!" he called. "I'll be there in a minute."

With the help of a pair of scissors he found in the desk drawer, he cut the rest of the twine and leaped from his chair. Hurrying back into the inner office, he switched on the lights and quickly released Vanessa and Joe.

"Joe," Vanessa asked anxiously, "are you all right?"

"It hurts like crazy," Joe said, reaching up to feel his wound, "but I guess I'll survive." He turned to Frank. "How did you get free?"

"I'll tell you later," Frank replied, picking up the phone on Zable's desk. "First, we have to warn Cooper."

"But how?" Vanessa asked. "He doesn't have a phone in the motor home."

Frank called Information and got the number of the Bayport Airfield. But when he dialed, all he got was a tape recording advertising the dates and times of the air races. He called Information again, but the operator couldn't locate another number.

With a frustrated groan, Frank slammed the phone down. "It's up to us. We have to find Cooper before he signs that contract." He turned to Joe. "Think you can make it to the car?"

"Definitely."

"Then let's get out of here," Vanessa said.

"Not so fast," Joe replied. With a grunt of pain, he walked to Zable's desk and took the Speedy Express contract from the bottom drawer. "*Now* we're ready to go."

Chapter

14

"CAN'T THIS VAN go any faster?" Joe asked impatiently.

"Not on this road," Frank said. The dirt road was riddled with potholes and had many blind turns. Glancing at the van's digital dashboard clock, Frank said, "Don't worry. This may be a back road, but it's the fastest way to the airport. We'll be there in twenty minutes, tops."

"What we should really do is drop Joe off at a hospital," Vanessa said.

"No way," Joe protested. "It's just a flesh wound. It's not even bleeding anymore."

Frank stared intently into the twilight as he steered the van around a winding curve. "I just hope Zable hasn't talked Cooper into signing that—"

131

His words were drowned out by the roar of a powerful airplane engine. Joe rolled down the passenger window and gazed up at the sky. "Hey, there's a plane flying over us," he said. "It can't be more than two hundred feet above the van."

Frank slowed down and looked for himself. It was a Mustang. In the twilight he could barely make out the colors—orange and white.

"It's the *Wild Child*," he said through clenched teeth.

"You mean Lyle Freemont's plane?" Vanessa asked with alarm.

Frank nodded. Although he knew it was pointless to try to lose the plane, he instinctively pressed the gas pedal.

Vanessa stared up at the *Wild Child*. "He's following us."

Suddenly, the landing gear descended from the belly of the Mustang. "Now what?" Joe muttered as the *Wild Child*'s nose dipped.

"Watch out!" Vanessa cried as the plane swooped down in front of the van.

At the last second, the plane lifted slightly. As it roared overhead, the wind from the propeller sent the van rocking to the left.

Vanessa shrieked, and Joe let out a low gasp. Skidding on two wheels, the van careened across the road. Frank yanked the steering wheel to the right and shot back onto the right side of the road.

"What's that idiot trying to do?" Joe cried.

"That's an easy one," Frank said. "He's trying to stop us from going back to the airfield and warning Cooper."

"But how did he know where we were?" Vanessa asked.

"Here he comes again!" Joe broke in.

The roar of the Mustang drowned out Joe's final words. Frank veered to the side of the road and slammed on the brakes. "Get out!" he shouted, throwing his door open.

Joe and Vanessa scrambled from the van. The *Wild Child* dove down on them like a monstrous bird of prey. With Frank close behind, Joe and Vanessa ran into the grassy field beside the road and fell to their stomachs.

An instant later, the Mustang thundered over the van. The wheels of the plane connected with the roof. The van tipped over and crashed onto its side.

Joe crawled to his knees and shook his fist at the departing airplane. "Come down here and fight us face-to-face, you coward!"

It was almost as if Freemont had heard Joe's words. The Mustang banked and headed back toward them. As it flew closer, Joe could see Freemont in his cowboy hat, sitting in the cockpit. The look on his face was one of cruel delight.

"Get down!" Frank yelled. He grabbed Joe's pants leg and pulled him into the grass.

Joe hit the ground with a grunt of pain, just

seconds before the Mustang thundered over them. The wind from the propeller threw grass and dirt into the air, and the wheels were so low they almost skidded across Joe's back.

"He's trying to kill us!" Vanessa cried.

"We're trapped," Frank shouted, thinking out loud. "The van is out of commission, and there's nowhere to hide in this open field."

Up in the sky, Freemont was circling back toward them.

"What are we going to do?" Vanessa asked anxiously.

"If we had a gun, we might be able to damage the rudder," Joe said.

"I've got an idea," Frank said. "Joe, we have jumper cables under the floor in the back of the van, don't we?"

Joe immediately realized what his brother had in mind. "Go for it," he said. "I'll keep Freemont busy."

Frank crawled on his stomach toward the van. Joe jumped to his feet and ran into the field, waving his good arm wildly in an effort to distract Freemont.

It worked. The Mustang changed course and roared down on Joe. At the last possible second, Joe clutched his shoulder and threw himself to the ground. The plane roared over him, leaving a mini hurricane in its wake.

Frank reached the van and immediately noticed a small black box wedged beneath the rear bumper. Looking it over, he recognized it as a remote-control homing device. "So *that's* how Freemont found us," he muttered. "The same way he found the *Beauty* . . ."

Quickly, Frank tossed the homing device aside and opened the van's rear doors. He reached inside and pulled open the storage compartment in the floor. Inside was a spare tire, a gasoline can, and a set of jumper cables. He grabbed the cables and ran back to the field.

The Mustang banked and headed toward him. Frank held the cables behind his back and shook his fist at the approaching plane. "Come and get me, Freemont!" he shouted.

The *Wild Child* roared toward him, no more than fifteen feet off the ground. As it approached, Frank swung the jumper cables like a lasso and flung them at the nose of the plane. They caught in the propeller and instantly wound around the blades.

With an ear-splitting grinding sound, the propeller slowed to a near halt. Instantly, the Mustang began to lose altitude.

His heart pounding, Frank threw himself out of the path of the oncoming airplane. Joe and Vanessa, a safe distance away, jumped up and ran toward the descending plane. Once the plane had passed him, Frank leaped up and followed.

The wheels of the Mustang hit the ground. The plane bumped across the grass, veering left and right, until finally it came to a halt in the middle of the field.

Frank, Joe, and Vanessa climbed onto the wing of the Mustang just as Freemont flung open the canopy. "Get back!" he ordered, reaching under the seat. He came up with a gun and pointed it at them.

Joe didn't hesitate. He brought his fists down against the top of the canopy, slamming it against Freemont's arm. With a gasp of surprise and pain, Freemont dropped the gun.

Frank snatched the gun out of the grass and threw it as far as he could. "Get out of the plane!" he commanded.

Freemont did as he was told. "Don't hurt me," he pleaded.

"I've got just the thing for you," Joe said. With Vanessa's help, he untangled the jumper cables from the *Wild Child*'s propeller and used them to tie Freemont's arms tightly behind his back. Then he tied his legs together.

"That hurts!" the pilot cried.

"After what you put us through, you should be thankful we don't tie you to the Mustang's landing gear and drag you back to Bayport," Joe said.

"What now?" Vanessa asked.

"I'll fly to the airfield and find Cooper," Frank said.

"If that lasso trick didn't damage the engine," Vanessa remarked.

"We won't know until we try it," Frank said. "Anyway, it's our only hope."

Joe nodded. "Here, take this," he said. He reached in his pocket and pulled out the contract between Zable Aviation and Speedy Express. "You might need it to convince Cooper that George Zable isn't such a good buddy after all."

Frank took the contract and put it in his shirt pocket. "Are you two going to be all right?"

"Sure," Joe said. "There's a house down the road. We'll use the phone there to call Con Riley and ask him to pick us up."

"What about me?" Freemont asked in a shaky voice.

Joe chuckled. "Oh, I'm sure Officer Riley will be happy to escort you to the Bayport police station."

Joe made sure that Freemont was tied securely before he and Vanessa headed toward the house to call the police.

Frank climbed into the *Wild Child* and started the engine. It coughed, stuttered, and finally managed a sputtering roar. The propeller was spinning, but it looked slightly lopsided.

Frank had no way of telling if the airplane was capable of taking off, or—assuming it could get airborne—if it would make it as far as the airfield.

He took a deep breath. "Well, here goes nothing." Crossing his fingers for luck, he pushed the throttle and started off across the dark, grassy field.

Chapter

15

FRANK CHECKED the console as the Mustang rose into the darkening sky. The engine was still coughing, and the temperature gauge showed that the plane was running hot. Frank decided to take it easy and not strain the engine any more than necessary. But that meant a longer flight—at least fifteen minutes total, he estimated.

Frank tapped his fingers impatiently against the joystick. He had to get there in time to stop Cooper from signing that contract. He just *had* to.

Frank's next problem was navigation. He knew how to fly the Mustang—well enough to fake it, anyway—but he had never flown this route before. The problem was compounded by the fact that the sun had set and the sky was almost black. Twinkling stars dotted the sky, mirrored by the twinkling lights that shone from the roads and houses below.

To stay out of the flight path of other air traffic, Frank decided to fly low and follow the main highway. It was wide and well lit, and from his vantage point it looked like a long, glowing serpent. It would lead him to Bayport, and from there he felt confident he could find the airfield.

He felt for the contract in his shirt pocket. If he could just get there in time . . .

At the edge of the field, Vanessa and Joe kept an eye on Freemont while they waited for the police. After a fifteen-minute wait, the sound of a siren split the night air. A police car appeared out of the darkness, its lights flashing. It was followed by a police tow truck.

The police car stopped, and Con Riley hopped out and strode through the field. "Are you all right, Joe?" he asked. "How is your wound?"

"It's just a scratch," Joe said, shrugging. "Freemont did it."

Riley turned to Freemont. "We've got a lovely cell waiting for you down at headquarters." He grabbed Freemont's arm and escorted him to the police car, then pushed him into the backseat. Joe and Vanessa watched as the van was hitched to the tow truck.

"Officer Riley, we have to get back to the

airfield right away," Vanessa said. "Can you take us?"

"Please," Joe said. "It's an emergency."

Riley thought it over for a moment. Then he said, "You'll be okay?"

Joe nodded, his face grave. Joe, Vanessa, and Riley climbed into the police car and started off down the dark country road with the lights flashing.

"Do you want to explain what's going on?" Riley asked

"Shooting Joe isn't all Lyle Freemont is responsible for," Vanessa said. "He's the one who sabotaged my Uncle Brett's plane."

"You've got proof of that?" Riley asked.

"Remember that tobacco you found on the seat of the *Killer Diller* after Cooper's plane was hedge-hopped?" Joe asked. "If you check it I think you'll find it's chewing tobacco—the same kind Freemont chews."

"Freemont did some of the dirty work," Vanessa added, "but George Zable masterminded the whole thing. His plan was to bankrupt Uncle Brett, and that creep succeeded. Zable's back at the airfield right now, trying to convince Uncle Brett to sign a contract giving up most of his rights to the *Beauty.*"

Riley shot through a red light, the siren screaming. "Not if we can help it," he said tersely.

* * *

Frank banked left, away from the highway. Below him, the lights of Bayport shimmered and twinkled. Flying low, he followed familiar roads and landmarks until he saw the airport in the distance.

Frank glanced at the temperature gauge. It had been in the red since he took off. Now the engine was emitting a high-pitched whine that sent butterflies fluttering through his stomach. Quickly, he flipped on the radio.

"*Wild Child* to Bayport Airfield control tower. I'm about two miles from the airfield, approaching from the southeast. Do you read me?"

"Control tower to *Wild Child*," a static-filled voice answered. "We've got you on the radar screen. Over."

"I'm flying hot and need to land immediately," Frank said. "Can you help me out? Over."

"We'll clear the landing field. Come on in."

Frank circled the airfield and lowered the landing gear. He followed the blue lights of the runway, touching down just as dark smoke began to billow from the engine.

As he taxied to a halt, a fire truck drove out to meet him. Frank leaped out of the cockpit just as the fire fighters opened their hoses on the Mustang's smoking fuselage.

Frank didn't wait around to see what would happen next. He jogged across the ramp to the

Beauty's pit. He found the plane illuminated by large floodlights, and Stan and Jesse working on the engines.

"Where's Cooper?" Frank asked.

"Don't know," Jesse replied. "Mr. Zable stopped by, and then they went off somewhere together."

"Do you know where?" Frank asked urgently.

Stan shrugged. "No idea. Why? Is something wrong?"

Frank didn't bother to answer. He took off across the ramp in the direction of the pilot's clubhouse. He ran through the downstairs rooms, searching for Cooper and Zable. All he found were a couple of pilots drinking beer at the bar.

Frank climbed the stairs two at a time and burst into the Sky High Coffee Shop. Five or six crew members were sitting at the counter, but Cooper and Zable were nowhere to be found.

"Has anyone seen Brett Cooper or George Zable?" Frank asked breathlessly.

The men shook their heads and went back to their coffee.

Frank ran outside and tried to think what to do next. Cooper and Zable could be anywhere on the ramp. Or they might have left the airfield and driven to Zable's house, his office, or a restaurant. The possibilities were endless.

The only thing to do, Frank decided, was to

stop at every pit on the ramp and ask if anyone had seen them.

Twenty minutes later, Frank had visited ten pits. No one had seen Cooper or Zable. Next stop was the *Wild Child*'s pit. Near the empty blacktop where the Mustang normally sat were Freemont's black Corvette, a white pickup truck, and a silver trailer. A light was on in the trailer.

Frank ran to the door and peered through the window. Inside Cooper and Zable were sitting at the kitchen table. Cooper's head was hanging low. He looked defeated and exhausted.

"You'll get a good salary and one percent of the profits," Frank heard Zable say. "Considering the mess you've gotten yourself into, I think that's pretty generous." Zable pointed to a stack of papers on the table and smiled. "Go on, Brett. Put your John Hancock right there. Then we can go out and celebrate."

Frank flung open the door and stepped inside. "Stop!" he cried. "Mr. Cooper, don't sign that!"

Zable's mouth fell open. "What the—" he began.

Frank ignored him and turned to Cooper. "Zable hired Cameron Diller and Lyle Freemont to sabotage your plane, Mr. Cooper. He even sent you defective parts and blackmailed you to stop racing. The plan was to bankrupt you so

143

you'd be forced to sign over the rights to the *Beauty*."

Cooper looked stunned. "What are you saying?"

"Look at this," Frank said, pulling the contract from his shirt pocket. "Zable signed a postdated contract with Speedy Express promising them he'd deliver two hundred Cooper-designed planes. He knew you'd have to work for him or risk bankruptcy because you couldn't pay your debts."

"That's enough," Zable said, reaching swiftly into his jacket pocket. When he pulled his hand out, he was holding the Browning automatic. He leveled it at Cooper. "Sign," he said.

"George, how could you?" Cooper asked. "I thought you were my friend. My *only* friend."

"Sign!"

Cooper picked up the pen. His hand was shaking. Slowly, he lowered the pen to the page and began to write.

Suddenly, something flew through the door of the trailer and hit Zable directly on the temple. As its sharp corner struck Zable's head, a puff of fine white powder filled the air, and Frank saw a five-pound box of cornstarch fall to the floor.

"Ow!" Zable cried, reaching up to clutch the side of his head.

It's now or never, Frank said to himself. He

tackled Zable around the waist and pulled him to the ground. The gun fell from his hand and clattered to the floor. Zable lunged for it, but Cooper stepped in and brought his boot down hard on Zable's wrist.

Zable grunted with pain and pulled his hand away. Quickly, Cooper reached down and grabbed the gun. He pointed it at Zable's forehead. "Don't move," Cooper ordered.

Zable froze. Frank jumped to his feet. Then he turned around to see who had thrown the box. Dixie was standing at the door of the trailer.

"Thanks," Frank said with a smile.

"I came over to see Lyle," Dixie explained, stepping into the trailer, "but when I looked in, I saw George pull a gun. So I ran to the pickup truck, grabbed the first thing I could find, and heaved it." She looked around, as if seeing everything for the first time. "What on earth is going on?"

"It's a long story," Frank said. "I'll explain later." He turned to Zable. "Stand up and step away from the table."

Zable got to his feet. But as he did, he slipped his fingers into his right cowboy boot.

Frank saw something metallic glint in Zable's hand. "Don't try it!" he shouted, stepping forward.

But it was too late. Zable lunged at Dixie. He

145

grabbed her around the waist and held a pearl-handled knife beneath her chin.

"Freeze," he warned, "or I'll slit her throat!"

"Do as he says," Dixie whispered, craning her chin away from the blade. A vein in her neck was throbbing, just millimeters from the sharp three-inch blade of Zable's knife.

Chapter

16

"IF YOU HURT HER, I'll kill you," Cooper said, his voice trembling with rage.

"Then stay in the trailer," Zable warned, "and don't call the cops."

He tightened his grasp on Dixie's waist and dragged her out of the trailer.

Frank and Cooper hurried to the door and watched helplessly as Zable opened the passenger door of Freemont's Corvette and pushed Dixie inside and over to the driver's seat. Zable, in the passenger side, held the knife to Dixie's throat. "Drive," he ordered.

A look of fear on her face, Dixie took off with the tires screeching.

As soon as the Corvette was out of sight, Frank turned to Cooper. "Where's your

jeep?'' he asked urgently. "We've got to follow them.''

"Forget the jeep," Cooper growled. "I have
a better idea.''

Con Riley's police car barreled through the
night, on its way toward the Bayport Airfield. In
the front seat, Joe sat between Riley and
Vanessa, staring impatiently out the windshield.
His wounded shoulder was throbbing, but he
barely noticed it.

A sign up ahead said Bayport Airfield, 1 Mile.
An arrow on the sign pointed left. Riley took the
corner at fifty miles per hour. Up ahead, the blue
lights of the airfield runway glowed in the darkness. Joe leaned forward in the seat, willing the
police car to go faster.

Suddenly, a black Corvette appeared up
ahead, zooming toward them at high speed. As
it approached, Joe noticed two people in the
front seat. He glanced at the license plate.

"LYL FLYS," he read. "That's Freemont's
car!''

"But he's here in the backseat," Riley said.

"It's got to be Zable," Joe said. "Turn
around! We have to stop him!''

Riley hit the brakes and spun the steering
wheel. The police car swung around, throwing
up gravel as it skidded onto the shoulder. Riley
stomped on the accelerator, and the car shot

down the road in hot pursuit of the black Corvette.

The distance between the police car and the Vette was shrinking. Suddenly the Corvette leaped forward as if it had shifted into warp drive.

Joe, Vanessa, and Riley watched as the Vette's tail lights receded into the darkness. "Can't you go any faster?" Joe urged.

"You'll never catch my Vette," Freemont said. "She's the road equivalent of the *Wild Child*—souped up and ready to race."

Joe slammed his fist against the dashboard. "We're going to lose him!"

At that moment, the growl of an airplane hit their ears. It grew louder until it became a roar. Vanessa rolled down the window and looked into the sky. "It's the *Beauty!*" she cried.

Joe leaned across her and looked for himself. *Brett's Beauty* was roaring overhead, a mere one hundred feet above the road. In the darkness, she looked like a pale white spaceship skimming the surface of the earth.

As Joe and Vanessa watched, the *Beauty* flew past them as effortlessly as if she were passing a tricycle. The plane continued on until it reached the black Corvette. Then it dipped down and buzzed the Vette.

The prop wash made the Corvette vibrate wildly. It skidded across the broken white line, swerving unsteadily.

* * *

Up in the *Beauty,* Frank and Cooper let out a whoop of joy.

"One more pass should do it," Cooper said with satisfaction.

"Don't fly too low," Frank warned. "You don't want to hurt Dixie."

"Don't worry. It won't take much more to scare Zable into letting Dixie stop. Underneath that tough-guy attitude, he's basically a wimp."

Cooper pushed the joystick, and the *Beauty*'s nose dipped. He thundered over the Corvette.

From the front seat of the police car, Joe and Vanessa watched the Vette shake violently under the *Beauty*'s prop wash. As the plane rose in the sky, the Corvette veered off the road, But instead of stopping, it barreled into the field. A second later, the headlights went off and the Vette disappeared into the darkness.

"Follow him!" Joe cried.

Riley didn't hesitate. He skidded off the road and drove into the field, veering left and right in an effort to locate the Corvette in the police car's headlights.

From their vantage point in the sky, Frank and Cooper stared in disbelief at the sudden darkness of the road.

"Where'd Zable go?" Cooper cried in frustration.

"Don't tell me we've lost them," Frank said.

Cooper and Frank searched frantically for a sign of the car.

Suddenly Frank said, "Look, there's a police car. It must be following the Vette. Maybe we'd better land and let the cops handle this."

"No way," Cooper barked. "I have an idea."

Cooper banked hard and maneuvered the *Beauty* across the field, flying so low that the wing lights acted as headlights, illuminating the field. "There they are," he muttered, pointing down at the Corvette as it zigzagged across the grass.

"Buzz them again," Frank said.

Cooper flew in low as if he were about to buzz the Vette. Instead, he lowered the landing gear and banked with so much force that he and Frank were pressed against the seat.

Suddenly, Frank understood what was happening. Cooper was about to land the *Beauty* right in front of the Corvette!

"Don't do it!" Frank shouted. "If Dixie can't stop in time, she'll be hurt."

"If anybody knows how to drive, it's Dixie," Cooper replied. "I have faith in her."

Steadily, Cooper brought the *Beauty* down. As the wheels touched the ground, he cut the engines and hit the brakes. The plane careened across the grass and came to a halt directly in the path of the speeding car.

Frank looked out of the canopy. The Vette was tearing toward the side of the plane. If it kept coming, it would smash into the left wing.

In the plane's wing lights, Frank could see the look of horror on Zable's face as he realized what was happening. He dropped the knife as Dixie yanked the steering wheel left and slammed on the brakes. The Corvette skidded sideways and came to a halt—just two feet from the *Beauty*'s wingtip.

The police car was right behind the Corvette. Riley hit the brakes and came to a stop with his front fender touching the rear of the Vette.

Zable leaped out of the Corvette and ran.

"Let's get him!" Joe cried.

Joe, Vanessa, and Riley jumped out of the police car and took off after Zable. Frank scrambled out of the *Beauty* and followed.

Joe was in the lead. He ran hard, his hightops slapping against the grass. He could see Zable's dark shape stumble around the side of the *Beauty* and hear his exhausted panting. With a quick burst of speed, Joe overtook him. Ignoring his throbbing shoulder, he tackled Zable around the waist and brought him down.

Seconds later, Frank, Vanessa, and Con Riley caught up with Joe. "Stand up and put your hands behind your head," Riley ordered, slapping handcuffs on Zable. "You're under arrest!"

While Riley led Zable back to the police car, Frank and Vanessa returned to the Corvette to find Dixie. Cooper was already there, helping her out of the car.

"Are you all right?" he asked.

"Yes, thanks to you." She smiled. "That was some impressive flying!"

"And that was some impressive driving!" he replied with a grin. Then he took her hand. "Dixie, I know I've treated you badly, and you had a perfect right to divorce me. But there was a reason why I was acting so crazy. George Zable blackmailed me to—"

Dixie pressed her fingers against Cooper's lips, silencing him. "Tell me later," she said softly. "When we're alone."

Cooper smiled and reached into his breast pocket.

"And no more of these filthy things," Dixie said, taking the pack of cigarettes from him and pocketing them. "If you want to keep winning races, you have to stay healthy."

Cooper chuckled and turned to Frank. "Think you can get back to the airfield without me? Dixie and I want to go for a ride."

"Sure, Mr. Cooper," Frank replied.

The whine of the *Beauty*'s engines split the air. Everyone turned to watch as Brett and Dixie Cooper flew off together into the night.

Less than twenty-four hours later, Frank, Joe, Vanessa, and Mrs. Bender stood in the pit, watching the *Beauty* take off. Beside them, Ray Kolinsky was talking happily with Stan and Jesse. After Cooper had learned the truth about Zable, he had apologized to Ray for firing him.

Frank was glad to see Ray back in his old job as crew chief, grinning like a schoolboy.

"Go get 'em, Brett," Ray said into his walkie talkie. "Show the world what the *Beauty* can do."

"Consider it done," Cooper radioed back.

Ray turned to the Hardys and Vanessa. "We've been working toward this moment for five long years."

"If the *Beauty* wins, do you think Uncle Brett can shake the rumors that his plane is unreliable?" Vanessa asked.

"Those rumors are dead," Ray said. "Everyone's talking about the fact that Zable and Freemont were arrested last night for sabotage, and for Diller's death. All that's left is for Brett to show them what the *Beauty*'s capable of."

"Ladies and gentlemen, it's a beautiful day for an air race," the announcer said over the loudspeakers. "Flying today in the Unlimited Gold race are Brett Cooper in *Brett's Beauty*, Bob Trancas in *Miss Minnie*, Jack Stoddart in the *Black Bumblebee*, and Bernie Petracca in the *Buzzcat*."

The crowd let out a cheer as the four planes lined up over the airfield behind the AT-6 that Jack Larsen, the race starter, flew. "Gentlemen," Larsen intoned, "you have a race!"

Frank watched as the Unlimiteds thundered toward the first pylon. The *Beauty* was in the lead and that's where she stayed. Throughout the race no one passed her—no one even came close. As she crossed the finish line, Frank let out a cheer. In the stands, the crowd leaped to its feet and screamed wildly.

"Brett's Beauty is number one," the announcer cried, "with a new piston-engine speed record of five hundred and twenty-two miles per hour!"

As soon as Cooper landed, he was surrounded by reporters, photographers, and aviation executives eager to make a deal. But Frank was pleased to see that Cooper brushed them all off and headed for Dixie's pit.

Frank and Joe watched the pilot climb into the back of the hot-pink biplane with Dixie and take off, circling high above the airfield. As the biplane passed the grandstand, a banner unfurled from the tail fin of the plane with the words *Just Married* printed across it.

"Married!" Frank gasped. "When did *that* happen?"

"Early this morning," Ray said with a grin. "They went to Bayport City Hall and demanded to be remarried on the spot."

"Wow!" Vanessa exclaimed. "Uncle Brett and Dixie must really be flying high."

Joe groaned at the bad joke, then added one of his own. "From today on, Brett and Dixie Cooper's future is unlimited!"

Frank and Joe's next case:

Trick or treat has turned to terror for the Hardy boys. Never before have they experienced a more horrific Halloween—a nightmare come true. First, it was Joe's friend Vanessa Bender . . . Then Frank's friend Callie Shaw . . . And now their own mother. Frank and Joe are the only witnesses to three shocking murders—and no one believes them!

Strange, unspeakable forces are loose in Bayport. Enemies the boys thought long dead have risen like demons to taunt and terrorize them. Now they stand alone in a titanic battle against an awesome, unknown power—a chilling army of evil determined to pursue them into the grave . . . or to the very edge of madness . . . in *Dead of Night,* Case #80 in The Hardy Boys Casefiles™.